Praise for T

"Fast-paced and engaging, *Trapped in the Cascades* converges three separate storylines, each ripe with malicious intent and life-threatening repercussions. These are woven into a nail-biting finale with Luke McCain and his faithful companion, Jack, fighting off dangerous weather conditions and the ticking timer towards death if they are unsuccessful. A five-star read!"

–J.C. Fuller, author of *The Rockfish Island Mysteries*

"I kept turning pages in *Trapped in the Cascades* long after I should have been doing other things, but as I followed Luke and Jack through biting winds and snow, smelling pine crushed underfoot and hearing the pop of pine sap from the fire, I couldn't put the book down. Phillips is a great storyteller who can weave clever mysteries and plot twists that particularly appeal to people who love the outdoors but will please anyone who likes a good thriller."

–Dalyn Weller, author of the *Apple Valley Ranchers series*

"I had almost given up reading novels ... then I picked up *Creature of the Cascades*. Here is something you don't see every day. Rob Phillips writes real places into this page-turner, and he is not averse to taking risks with humor, suspense and wordplay. I was hooked from the first jump."

–Gary Lewis, TV host and author of *Fishing Central Oregon, Fishing Mount Hood Country*, and *John Nosler Going Ballistic*

"Rob Phillips takes you on another fun romp into the wilds of Washington State as Luke McCain works ... to figure out who or what is killing pets, livestock, and wild game in the South Cascades. Is it Sasquatch as some believe or is it something else?"

–John Kruse, host of *Northwestern Outdoors* and *America Outdoors Radio*

"*Cascade Manhunt* is the fifth book of Rob Phillips' Luke McCain series, and I believe it to be his best work . . . . As a retired Washington

State undercover Fish and Wildlife detective, I found Rob's book to be spot-on. I simply couldn't put *Cascade Manhunt* down and am already thirsting for Rob's next book."

–Todd Vandivert, retired Washington State Fish and Wildlife detective and author of the Wildlife Justice series

"Poaching big game . . . check. A loveable yellow Lab . . . double check. Computer hackers from India . . . WHAT! That last item is the big checklist twist in outdoor writer Rob Phillips' latest novel, *Cascade Kidnapping*, the fourth in his Luke McCain series. As in all of Phillips' books, *Cascade Kidnapping* reinforces healthy respect for the outdoors and laws that protect it."

–Bob Crider, retired editor and publisher, *Yakima Herald-Republic*

"This is crime fiction at its finest–the perfect blend of a compelling mystery, a fabulous setting, the best dog ever, and a very likeable hero you won't forget."

–Christine Carbo, award-winning author of the Glacier Mystery Series

"*Cascade Vengeance* takes readers on a thrill ride through the dual worlds of drug dealing and big-game hunting deep in Washington's Cascade mountains. Rob Phillips uses his extensive knowledge of the region to tell the fast-moving tale . . . on the way to the story's harrowing and heartbreaking conclusion."

–Scott Graham, National Outdoor Book Award-winning author of *Mesa Verde Victim*

"*Cascade Vengeance*, the second book in the Luke McCain series, is another hang-onto-your-hat, nonstop action episode with Luke, a Washington State Fish and Wildlife officer, his FBI girlfriend Sara, and Jack, his loyal yellow Lab. I felt like I was riding shotgun in Luke's Ford pickup, bouncing along forest service roads where very bad guys might be lurking."

–Susan Richmond, owner of Inklings Bookshop

TRAPPED IN THE CASCADES

Book and cover design by Kevin Breen

ISBN: 978-1-957607-31-3
Cataloging-in-Publication Data is available upon request

Manufactured in the United States of America

Published by
Latah Books, Spokane, Washington
www.latahbooks.com

The author may be contacted at yakimahunter@yahoo.com

TRAPPED IN THE CASCADES

A LUKE MCCAIN NOVEL

ROB PHILLIPS

LATAH
BOOKS

Also by Rob Phillips

THE CASCADE KILLER

CASCADE VENGEANCE

CASCADE PREDATOR

CASCADE KIDNAPPING

CASCADE MANHUNT

CREATURE OF THE CASCADES

A DOG LIFE WELL LIVED

CHAPTER 1

The first signs of the snowstorm began as an occasional big, fluffy flake. They floated out of the steel gray sky as pretty as a picture. One feathery flake here, another downy flake there.

Steve Reid saw the snow coming. He had been watching a wall of white moving in from the west for the past twenty minutes, and when the large flakes started fluttering down around him, he picked up his pace.

Reid, who was fifty-two years old and in excellent shape from hiking in the mountains throughout the years, had set his trapline high up along a creek in a small watershed near the crest of the Cascades and he needed to check three more traps before he could turn around and head back to his truck. He had set his line of ten traps two days earlier, when there was already six inches of snow on the ground from a storm the previous week. The snow had settled some, giving a hint of the trail he needed to be on, so, for the time being, it was fairly easy to navigate.

After watching the weather reports early that morning, Reid knew there was another storm circling around from the Gulf of Alaska that would be hitting the Cascades at some point, so he had come prepared. He had been caught in snowstorms before and he'd learned the hard way that even though they were somewhat cumbersome to pack, snowshoes and a waterproof coat should be carried just in case.

Reid watched as the fluffy flakes multiplied by the second. Within five minutes, the snow was falling so heavily he could hardly see the trail five feet in front of him. Still, because he knew the country—he'd trapped this drainage for the past four years—he marched on, determined to check the last of his traps to make sure he collected all the animals he may have caught. He stopped, dropped his pack, pulled out the waterproof coat, put it on, and continued up to the next trap.

Five of the first eight traps Reid checked were empty, but the other three had successfully captured two martens and a bobcat. After dispatching them with a quick shot from his pistol, he placed the three animals in a tree along the trail and would pick them up on his hike back down to his rig. No sense in packing the animals up the hill and back down again.

The canopy of evergreens slowed some of the falling snow, but the flakes eventually fought their way through the branches and continued piling up quickly. The heavy snowfall pushed Reid to move up the trail faster, doubling his normal walking speed. He had a half mile to go to the next trap, and another half mile to reach the last one. If he didn't get to them and they had caught something, it was a good bet that he would lose his catch to coyotes or a cougar.

Because he was in a hurry, and because the snow was falling so fast and heavy it was blocking his vision, he didn't see the trouble he was about to get into. Reid wiped his face continually and wished he had brought his ski goggles.

As he approached the ninth trap, a set for marten up against the trunk of a fir tree and covered in grass and brush, he looked to see if the cage trap was occupied. He couldn't see anything in the trap and stepped closer to pull it away from the tree trunk.

The instant his foot hit something hard in the soft snow, depressing the trigger pan, he knew what it was, but he wasn't quick enough to pull his leg back. In a split second, the Sawtooth bear trap snapped shut on Reid's leg, hitting his lower calf just above his boot top. One of the sharpened teeth on the jaws of the trap pierced his leg, breaking the fibula and cracking the tibia bone.

Without looking down, Reid knew what had happened, but he couldn't figure out why. Bear trapping with a leghold trap in Washington State had been outlawed years ago, so he didn't just happen into someone's bear trap. Had someone intentionally placed the trap here to catch him?

His leg hurt, but nothing like it was going to hurt later, he knew. Reid carefully pulled on the heavy chain that was attached to the trap, trying not to move the steel contraption and risk further damage to his leg. The chain popped up out of the new-fallen snow and led to the trunk of a big pine tree about six feet away. He could see it was wrapped around the tree and had been secured back onto itself with an industrial-sized combination padlock.

Trying to pull the jaws of the trap apart with his hands was useless. First, he couldn't get a good angle on the thing, and his hands were shaking. Still, he tried. Although he had never used one before, Reid was familiar with these traps and knew that if he was ever going to get out of it, he would have to spread the jaws to allow his leg to slide out. Most trappers using such big traps carried a steel bar or some other tool to help pry the jaws apart. Reid had no such thing but figured a sturdy stick would do the job. He looked around, but with the fresh snow, saw nothing that might work.

Then he remembered his snowshoes. His were traditional-style snowshoes, handmade from wood, with a long tail where the two sides of the frame came together in the back. Pulling his pack off his back, which was normally second nature, suddenly became a chore. Just the slight twist of his body sent a lightning bolt up his leg.

Reid had seen all kinds of trauma as a medic in the Army while fighting in Iraq. He had seen soldiers succumb from going into shock. He knew he needed to stay calm, so after the jolt of pain subsided, he took a deep breath and slowly removed the backpack. The snowshoes were tied to the pack, and he untied and removed them.

He wanted to sit down but decided that to get enough leverage on the jaws of the trap, he would need to come at them from the top, and he would have more strength while standing. Plus, moving to sit down would most assuredly hurt like hell.

Again, Reid paused and took a deep breath. The pain in his leg was intensifying. He tried not to let in any thoughts of what might happen if he couldn't free his leg from the trap.

His first attempt at prying the jaws of the trap open was almost successful. Reid was able to work the jaws apart just enough that his ankle and foot could pass through it. The problem was the three-inch tooth on the trap that had impaled his leg kept him from moving his foot. He didn't realize he was stuck on the tooth until the second he tried to pull his leg free. Nothing moved, and another bolt of pain jumped up his leg.

"DAMMIT!" Reid screamed out of frustration and pain.

On his next try to pry open the jaws of the trap, the tail end of the snowshoe broke. When it did, it seemed to push the tooth on the trap even deeper into his leg.

The pain now was almost unbearable, yet Reid knew he must persist. With the snow piling up so quickly and the remoteness of his location on the mountain, this could quickly become a life-and-death situation.

His wife knew he was up in the Taneum, but like many trappers, Reid had been secretive about the precise location of his traplines. None of his family members or trapping buddies knew exactly where he was. They might have an idea, but they didn't know for sure.

Reid wondered how in the hell someone knew about him trapping up here. And who would set such a deadly trap.

He shook it off. There was no time to think about that now. He had to free himself from the trap and get back down the mountain to his truck.

With the second snowshoe in his shaking hands, Reid stuck the tail of the shoe into the gap between the jaws holding his leg and worked the upper part of the snowshoe away from his body, slowly prying the two jaws apart. If he could get the trap open wide enough, then he would have to figure out how to work his leg off the tooth and then out of the trap.

When the tail of the second snowshoe broke, the trap snapped back almost as hard as when Reid had first stepped in it. The first time, the leg had hurt. This time the pain was unbelievable. He felt himself getting sick and woozy, and in the next second he passed out.

*

Sam Anderson also saw the snow coming. He was almost to the end of his line and had one more trap to check. Not wanting to get caught in the snowstorm, Anderson hurried along. When he was seventy yards from his final trap, one he'd hoped would capture a bobcat, he stopped and pulled his binoculars from the carrier on his chest.

The tall, lanky Anderson often checked his traps with binoculars for a couple reasons. First, it saved him the walk to the last trap, which in the grand scheme of things was no big deal. The main reason he did it was that if there was nothing in the trap, he wouldn't need to walk up to it and spread any human scent around the area.

Anderson looked at the trap and saw that nothing was in it. Then he caught something out of the corner of his eye. Something seemed out of place. He focused the binos on the base of a twenty-five-foot-tall fir tree a few feet from his trap and saw a chain wrapped around it.

"What the hell?" Anderson mumbled to himself.

He had been using this trapping site for many years and never had seen a chain around that tree before. He had sat under that tree two weeks earlier to wait out a rain squall and certainly would have seen a big chain like that.

Anderson's father had been a trapper. And as a boy he had been with his dad when he had trapped a couple of black bears. As soon as Anderson saw the chain, he knew what it was. Someone had set a leghold trap and chained it to the tree. He cautiously moved ahead and walked off the trail to get to the tree. He grabbed the chain at the tree and slowly pulled it up. The chain was hidden in the brush and packed into a few inches of loose snow, but because Anderson knew what to look for it was pretty obvious.

He followed the chain with his eyes and then spotted the big black metal trap hiding in the snow on the trail. Someone had tried to camouflage it with the snow, but it was obviously the work of amateurs.

With the end of an eight-foot log he scrounged up nearby, Anderson dropped it on the trap, and the thing snapped closed, breaking the rotting wood into pieces.

He was happy he had not stepped into the trap, for sure, and he began thinking about who had set it there and why someone might do that. Trapping bears was illegal. So were leghold traps. So it wasn't a legit trapper. Could some renegade trapper have been targeting a bear or cougar that might be attracted to his trap? Or—and this made no sense to him at all—could someone be targeting *him*?

No time to stand around thinking about it. Since he had no way of removing it from the fir tree, Anderson pulled the sprung trap and chain back to the tree, slung the trap up and over a branch next to the trunk, and turned back to head down the trail. Before he reached his truck, the first few flakes of the storm started floating out of the sky. By the time he got to the road where his truck was parked, there was already an inch of snow covering the vehicle.

✳

Ninety-two minutes before Reid stepped into the trap, a green Subaru Outback drove up the Forest Service road and stopped next to Reid's pickup where it was parked near a game trail that headed up a creek.

"He's up the trail," said a young woman driving the car. "You think we're going to get him?"

"I don't know," a man sitting in the passenger seat of the Subaru said. "We put it in the right spot, and if he's not looking for it, I think we can get him. Plus, it looks like it's going to snow, so that should help camouflage the trap."

"Good," the woman said. "Let's go check on the others."

She turned the smaller SUV around and headed back down the rough road. When she saw that her cell phone finally had reception, she pulled up a name and pushed the call button.

"Is he on the trail?" the woman who answered the phone asked.

"Yes," the woman said. "How about your guy?"

"Yes."

"Meet at the apartment in two hours as planned."

"Will do," the woman said, and she was gone.

"Is their guy on the trail?" the man in the passenger seat asked.

"Melissa said he is," the woman said. "They're heading to meet us at the apartment."

"Man, I wish I could be there when that asshole steps in that trap," the man said. "To see the fear in his face would be the perfect payoff."

The woman didn't say anything. She hated cruelty and violence of any kind, but especially to animals. She believed in what they were doing, but she didn't need to see the man get caught in the trap. Just knowing he might get caught, which would hopefully stop his horrible pursuit of poor, defenseless creatures just for their hides, was good enough for her.

She knew there was a slight possibility that what they were doing might lead to the death of one of the trappers on their hit list, so she tried not to think about it. But she did. In fact, with the impending snowstorm she thought about it even more.

After a few minutes, she asked, "You think he'll be able to get out of the trap if he steps in it?"

"I would guess so," the man in the passenger seat said. "Those guys all know their way around a trap."

"Yeah, but that was a damn big bear trap," she said with a worried tone in her voice. "And with the big storm they're talking about, he could die if he can't get out of it."

"Listen, Maddy. We've gone around and around on this. The trap itself will not kill anyone. But if he can't get out of it, well, yeah, there is always the possibility he might die."

"Oh, I don't want to hear that."

"Again, we discussed all the possibilities, and everyone agreed. Now you're having second thoughts?"

"I want the guy to suffer just like the animals he traps, but I don't want him to die."

"Kinda too late for that," the man said.

"We could go back up there, hike in, and check on him," she said. "If he can't get out, we could be the heroes, coming in to save the day."

"How would we explain that? Just a nice couple out hiking on some trail that no one has ever heard of."

"If he's stuck in the trap, he wouldn't care where we came from."

"Sooner or later, he would figure it out. I say we let it be and go meet up with the others."

Maddy didn't say anything else and kept driving. But she didn't stop thinking about the trapper and what might happen if he were to die up there with his leg caught in the trap.

CHAPTER 2

Luke McCain looked through the windshield of his Chevy pickup and watched as the fluffy white flakes transitioned from a beautiful winter scene into a near whiteout.

"We better get down the hill," Luke said to his yellow Labrador retriever, Jack, who often rode with him as he patrolled the mountains of Central Washington. "This is getting ugly."

As a veteran police officer with the Washington State Department of Fish and Wildlife or WDFW, it was Luke's job to make sure everyone, particularly hunters and anglers, were following the rules as they enjoyed their pursuits in the region.

Over the years, Luke, with Jack's help, had run down two different serial killers, a growing number of poachers, and had been in a shootout with a suspect during an investigation that involved what many believed to be bigfoot.

The weather girl on the TV news that morning, using colorful maps and a computer-generated storm path prediction, said a snowstorm was approaching the region, but her estimate of its arrival had been about twelve hours off. According to the slender and smiling blonde on the tube, who Luke thought might be all of nineteen years old, the bulk of the snow wasn't supposed to reach the area until after midnight, and it wasn't supposed to be more than five or six inches of accumulation.

The way the snow was falling now, it might reach a foot or more in a few hours. And if it kept snowing, who knew how deep it might get.

"Wrong again, Tiffany," Luke said to no one in particular as his windshield wipers whipped back and forth, barely keeping the glass clean enough to allow him to see what had only minutes before been an obvious road.

He looked over his shoulder at the yellow dog curled up asleep on the back seat and realized that Jack didn't give one hoot about what the weather was doing outside, or how badly the weather person had screwed up.

Luke had checked several hunters earlier in the day. All had the appropriate licenses and tags. None had had any success in finding a yearling spike bull, the only animal hunters with a general elk tag in their pocket were legally able to take east of Washington's Cascade Mountains during the general rifle elk season.

His plan had been to start out early in the day up in the Taneum, south and west of Cle Elum, and then work his way down to another game management unit in the afternoon. But because he had run into several groups of hunters, he was still in the highest portion of his patrol area in the Cascades when the snow started to fall.

As a twenty-two-year veteran with WDFW, Luke had spent hours and hours driving the roads in the Central Cascades during every month of the year, and he had faced some bad roads many times. But as he watched the snow coming down in sheets and noticed that it had filled his tire tracks made only a few minutes before when he had driven up the road to find a place to turn around, he could only remember a couple times being in snow falling this heavily.

The state-issued truck that Luke drove had good tires and four-wheel drive, so he felt comfortable driving in deep snow. And he had chains for all four tires if he needed them. Only once had he had to resort to chaining up all fours, and that was to help pull a hunter's rig out of a deep snowdrift in a bar ditch three years before. Luke thought about the chains and what a pain they were to put on and hoped he wouldn't have to use them.

He was concentrating on the road, which was not easy, being it was all white in a sea of white, when his radio crackled.

"Wildlife 148, this is Wildlife 127. Come in."

Luke jumped at the sound of the radio and quickly grabbed the mic.

"Yeah, go ahead, 127."

Normally, the other game wardens would just use their names when calling each other, but for some reason fellow officer Stan Hargraves was using official protocol on this call.

"Where are you, Luke?"

"I'm in a full-blown whiteout in the Taneum. What's up?"

"I'm over above Rimrock Lake, dealing with a poaching situation and could use some help."

"Sorry, Stan, but in this snow, I'm a good three hours away."

"Okay, I'll stay in touch."

"Is it snowing up where you are?" Luke asked.

"Yes, sir," Hargraves said. "It's snowing hard and piling up fast. I'm going to strangle that weather girl from the morning TV."

"That thought had crossed my mind too," Luke said. "But we both know better than to trust those forecasts."

"Yeah, and it wouldn't have stopped us anyway, probably."

"It might have kept me in the lower elevations. It has snowed three inches in just fifteen minutes here."

"I'm worried this is going to strand some hunters," Hargraves said. "I checked some guys camped down in a hole this morning.

If it keeps up at this pace, they're never going to get out of there. Hopefully, they were smart enough to pack up and get out when the snow started."

"I wouldn't bet on it," Luke said. "You know how some of those guys are."

Over the years Luke had checked on thousands of hunters, and in his mind elk hunters in general were the most dedicated, and some were more than fanatical about trying to notch their tags.

"Roger that," Hargraves said. "Stay in touch."

"Will do," Luke said. "Wildlife 148, clear."

Twice on the way down through the mountains Luke spotted trucks at elk camps, and he pulled in, more to make sure what their plans were than to check on their licenses and hunting success.

No one was around at the first camp, which was made up of a twenty-foot travel trailer. Luke knocked on the door, but there was no answer. The pickup truck, a mid-2000s Chevy 2500 four-by-four parked at the trailer, was covered in snow, so either the hunters were out hunting in another truck or they were possibly in an ATV. Luke looked around and saw there was no trailer that would have been needed to haul a side-by-side up the mountain, so it was more likely the hunters had taken off on foot that morning.

Luke jumped back in his pickup and waited for a bit to see if he saw anyone walking into camp, but as the snow continued to pile up, he decided he needed to keep moving down the mountain.

The second camp he came to had a giant wall tent, with a Jeep and a Nissan pickup parked nearby. Gray smoke was fighting its way through the snow out of a rusty brown chimney that was poking out of the top of one side of the tent.

Luke pulled in, left the truck running, jumped out, turned his coat collar up against the wet snow, and started for the tent.

"Hello to the camp?" Luke hollered as he walked to the zippered door at the end of the tent.

"Yeah, come on in," a husky voice answered.

Luke knelt, searched for the zipper puller in the fresh snow, found it, and pulled it up to open the canvas door.

"Hi, fellas," Luke said to three men, all of whom looked to be in their fifties, sitting in fold-out lawn chairs next to a crackling fire in a small woodstove.

As a police officer with the Washington State Department of Fish and Wildlife, Luke was an imposing figure. He stood just short of six foot five and was a very fit 224 pounds. With the badge on his coat and his pistol in its holster on his utility belt, he was quickly recognized as a game warden.

"Hello, marshal," the most rotund of the three men said. He had a round, red face and was mostly bald on top with some scraggly gray hairs sticking up in all directions like he had just woke up from a nap. "Grab a chair. We have some hot coffee here if you'd like a cup."

"No thanks," Luke said. "I can't stay long. Just wanted to check in and see what your plans are, what with this storm blowing in all of a sudden."

A second man, also a little overweight and still wearing a down hunting coat with a fluorescent orange vest over the top of it, said, "We were just discussing that. We're thinking we might just ride it out."

"If all the other jokers around here get all worried and head out, it should be better hunting for us once the snow stops," said the third man who looked to be the most fit of the three and had a full thick brown beard. A bright orange crusher hat was pulled down almost over his eyes.

Luke looked at the man and figured if he had to identify him later, he had no idea what the man really looked like.

"I don't see any meat on the pole out there," Luke said. "So I assume you've not had any luck?"

"No, sir," the bearded man said. "We seen a bunch of cows up the road a mile or so, and two big six-points, but no spikes."

"There's elk around," said the red-faced man who was wearing gray sweatpants, slip-on rubber boots, and a University of Idaho hoodie. "We just need to find the right one."

"You all from around here?" Luke asked.

"Me and Frank are from the Tri-Cities, and Lonnie there," the man in the U of I sweatshirt said as he pointed his coffee cup at the man in the orange vest, "he's from Spokane."

"Okay," Luke said as he looked around the tent. He saw three rifles leaned up against a crossbar in the tent which meant the three men were all most likely hunting. "If you'll show me your hunting licenses, I'll get out of your hair."

The three men all reached for their wallets, started digging paper out, and handed their licenses to Luke. He looked them over quickly, making sure they were all legal, and handed them back.

"Everything looks good," Luke said. "But you might think about getting out of here if this snow continues."

"Aw, we'll be fine," the man named Lonnie said. "We have enough food to feed the first infantry, and Frank cut enough firewood for a month, so we'll do alright."

"Suit yourself," Luke said and turned to go back out the tent door. "Good luck to you guys."

He wanted to say something about the amount of snow that had already built up on the roof of the tent but decided the men surely were experienced enough to keep an eye on it.

Just for the heck of it, when he climbed into the warmth of the truck cab, Luke pulled out the small tablet he always carried in his shirt pocket and wrote down the names of the three men. If he got a call later that a group of hunters had not been heard from in days, he would know where these three were camped if they were the missing hunters.

That done, he put the truck in gear and started down the road, wipers struggling against the never-ending snow.

He'd gone only two miles down the road when his radio crackled again.

"Wildlife 148, are you still up in the Taneum?"

"Yes, I am."

"We just got a call from a woman named Jessie Meyers looking for you. Says she's your neighbor."

"She is," Luke said. "What did she want?"

"Evidently, her son Austin and a friend were up camping somewhere near that unit, hunting elk, and he was supposed to be home last night. He didn't show up. She's worried that he or his buddy might be lost or hurt."

"She can't raise him on his phone?" Luke asked and immediately thought it was a stupid question. If Jessie could reach her son, she'd know where he was and if he was okay.

"She says she's called two dozen times, but it goes right to voicemail."

"Okay, I'll get into cell service down the hill and give her a call."

"Roger that."

As Luke drove down the road to a spot where he knew he could get phone service, he thought about Austin. Luke had been very involved with the young man as he was growing up. He had taught Austin, who lived across the street from him, how to fish in the rivers around the area. He had also helped the boy get through the hunter's safety course so he could get his hunting license.

Luke had been with Austin when he shot his first duck, and his first pheasant. And he had helped Austin pick out his first car. Those were all times when a father should have been there, but Austin's dad had divorced Jessie when Austin was about ten and hadn't been around much, so Luke had taken the boy under his wing.

Austin was now a freshman at Yakima Valley College, and for the past few years he had been doing more things with friends his age versus spending time with Luke. Austin had gotten into big game hunting, and after taking a nice mule deer buck the year before, Austin's goal, he told Luke, was to shoot an elk.

Luke was thinking about all that when his phone rang. He looked at the caller ID and saw it was Austin's mom calling.

"Hi, Jessie," Luke said. "I was just going to call you."

"I haven't heard from Austin. He was supposed to be home last night because he has classes today. I try not to worry about him, but you know how it is."

ROB PHILLIPS

"I do," Luke said. "He or his buddy probably shot an elk last night and they're packing it out today. I'm sure they are okay."

"I didn't know who else to call," Jessie said. "What do you think I should do?"

"All you can do is wait for a call from him," Luke said. "But I'll do some checking. You think he is hunting up in the mountains west of Cle Elum?"

"He told me they were going to be camping in the mountains up off I-90. I don't know what the area is called, but he said they were going to be pretty high up because that's where they had been seeing elk when they were doing their scouting."

"Are they in a tent, or did his friend have a camper or trailer?"

"I'm not sure. I think Austin was just going to sleep in the back of his truck."

Luke was familiar with Austin's latest truck, a white F-250 Ford pickup with a gray canopy covering the bed. The two-tone color created by the unmatching canopy always made it stand out in a sea of white Ford pickups.

"Okay," Luke said. "I'll see what I can do. Have you talked to Austin's friend's parents?"

"I talked to his mom earlier this morning, and she wasn't too worried. She was going to call me if she heard anything from her son."

"Is it snowing in Yakima?" Luke asked.

"No, but the weather girl said it wasn't going to start until later tonight."

Luke hesitated to tell Jessie that it was a major whiteout in the mountains, which was going to make it more difficult to find Austin if indeed he was lost or hurt.

"Okay," Luke said. "Try not to worry. And if you hear from Austin, give me a call, or have him call me."

Jessie Meyers said she would do that and said goodbye. Luke could hear the worry in her voice.

Trying to find someone, anyone, in this weather was going to be next to impossible, and not knowing exactly where Austin and his friend were hunting was going to make it even more difficult.

Since he had already checked all the camps up this road, Luke put the truck in gear and continued working his way down the mountain.

CHAPTER 3

Melissa Short had been an animal lover her whole life. When she was six, she found a scruffy orange and white kitten in a field near her house, and after much negotiating with her parents, they allowed her to keep it. Part of Short's deal with her folks was she was to care for the kitten, including feeding it daily, making sure it had water, and grooming it when necessary. She named the kitten Creamsicle but called it "Creme." Two more cats joined the family over the years, and Short was their caregiver as well. She loved her cats, and they loved her.

One day, as she walked home from junior high school, Short heard the meowing of a cat in a culvert under the road. She went down and found a dirty black and white cat caught in a small trap, both of its back legs crushed.

Short immediately freed the cat and carried it home in hopes that her mom would take it to the veterinarian to get medical help. When they got the cat to the vet's office, the doctor gave it a quick examination and told Short and her mother there wasn't anything she could do for it.

"The spine is broken, and the cat will never walk again," the vet explained to Short and her mother. "The most humane thing to do is to put it to sleep and end its suffering."

Short didn't want the cat to suffer, so they agreed to have it euthanized.

On the drive home, with the cat's remains in a box in the back seat, Short's mother said, "I know that was hard, but it was the right thing to do. We'll give it a nice burial in the field where you found Creme."

"Why would someone trap a cat?" Short asked.

"I don't think anyone was trying to catch a cat," her mother said. "The trap was probably set for a skunk or a muskrat."

"That's a terrible way to die for any animal," Short said.

*

Despite what her name might suggest, Short grew into a tall, slender woman, just over six foot, with long, mousey brown hair that fell to the top of her butt. Most of the time the hair was balled up into a bun that migrated around her head. Sometimes it was on top. Sometimes it was in the middle. And sometimes it was in the far back. Occasionally, when she had the time, she would braid her hair into a rope-like ponytail.

Her hazel eyes turned green in the sunlight, and she had eleven studs in her right ear, running from the top-right down to the bottom of the lobe. Her left ear only had seven piercings, including two inside the ear.

Short had long legs, long arms, long toes, and long fingers. Her face was slim, so while it wasn't long per se, it looked long, like the rest of her. Nothing about Short matched her surname. She was the living, breathing personification of contradiction.

One day, during a break from her studies at Central Washington

University in Ellensburg, she was checking out websites for like-minded animal lovers when Short came across a group that seemed very aggressive in their attitudes toward anything that might hurt or kill an animal. The group's website railed against pet shelters that euthanized dogs and cats and indicated they were doing everything they could to stop all hunting and trapping. Short had seen similar websites, but her attention was piqued by this group's focus on shutting down trapping. There was a contact number on the website, so she called it.

After talking with what sounded like a very angry and snobbish woman in Minnesota, Short received an email package that included information on the group—simply called STOP. She didn't know if that was an acronym for something or not because nothing was included. The group's mission statement listed twenty-seven things they wanted to stop, including the inhumane treatment of all animals, drug testing on all animals, hunting of all animals, trapping of all animals, and the list went on.

The package also included white papers on several subjects, including how archaic hunting had become. One white paper was titled "Haven't We Evolved Beyond Hunting for Pleasure?" Another paper questioned why the U.S. government wasn't funding only shelters that didn't kill animals. There were photos of news clippings from *The New York Times*, *The Washington Post*, and *The Los Angeles Times* about groups that had had success in changing practices in logging, the use of pesticides in farming, and other environmental issues. At the bottom of each of the clippings, someone—probably the angry woman in Minnesota—had written: WE CAN DO IT TOO! in red felt tip ink.

Short was on board with all the things STOP wanted to halt, but she was specifically interested in doing away with trapping. It was the twenty-first century for God's sake. Clothing was being made of space-age materials. Why in the hell would anyone need to kill an innocent animal for its fur?

One of the white papers in the package detailed a plan that would punish people who trapped innocent animals by giving them a taste of their own medicine. It involved following known trappers, learning where they set their traps, and then setting a trap for them.

"Once a person feels the pain and torture of having their leg end up in a trap, the chances of them trapping again are diminished considerably," the paper read.

The paper detailed how to go about getting the traps, how to set them, where to put them, and how to camouflage them.

One of Short's best friends, Madeline Haskins, had told her about an experience she'd had with her father who ran a pest control business and often trapped small animals that were being a nuisance or a danger to people or their pets. Even though trapping had put food on the table for her formative years, Haskins did not like trapping, and Short believed Maddy would help if they were to move ahead with a plan to try to stop trapping in the area around Ellensburg.

Haskins was eight inches shorter than Short, wore her blonde hair in a bob cut, and had a tiny gold hoop sticking out of the right nostril of her pudgy nose. Slightly overweight, with thick glasses in big round black frames, people thought she resembled a bug.

When she was little, Haskins had gone with her father when he set some traps. She loved her father dearly, but the first time she saw him dispatch a racoon that had been in one of his traps by smacking it on the head with the blunt end of a hatchet she got physically ill and swore she would never join him again.

Haskin's father tried to explain that trapping was something that had been going on for centuries, and the racoon he trapped had been killing a farmer's chickens and breaking all the eggs in their nests. The farmer raised the chickens and sold the eggs to help feed his family. The racoon was stealing from the family, and the only way to get it to stop was to eliminate it.

Still, the idea of killing an animal like that upset her to no end. She'd had bad dreams about it, with one recurring nightmare featuring some strange man coming after her with a hatchet.

Because of all that, Haskins was fine with trying to stop all trapping, but she wasn't sure this was the best way to do it.

"We've talked it through fifty times, Maddy," Short said curtly. "We'll be fine. No one will ever know we were the ones who did this. So, are you in or out?"

"I'm in, but I'm nervous. Is everyone else still a go?"

"Yes. I heard from the Prez a while ago. He's gung-ho."

"Of course," Haskins said. "I'm sure he thinks this is a way to get into your pants. Or mine."

"I don't know," Short said. "I think he really believes in the cause."

"Yeah, if the cause is to have sex with an actual girl."

"Let's not worry about that right now," Short said. "We have work to do."

Richard "Rick" Nixon, a perennial senior at Central Washington University who was currently working on his fourth undergraduate degree, had been willing to participate in Short's plan from the second he heard it.

Known around campus as "the Prez," Nixon was of average height and build, had a thin face with small, slightly yellow teeth, and wore his black hair 1970s long, which most of the time covered dime-sized black gages in his earlobes. A scraggly beard made him look like a potential homeless person, especially when he wore an old green Army jacket, which was most of the time.

The fourth member of the group was Skyler Loots. A big man, Loots looked a little like the blond Russian dude who fought Sylvester Stallone in *Rocky III*, or was it *Rocky IV*? He was twenty years old, six and a half feet tall, naturally muscular, and as strong as an ox. He had been a perfect addition to the group, Short thought, because in addition to the muscles in his arms and legs, his head was one big muscle.

"I don't think his antenna picks up all the channels," Haskins said when chatting with Short about Loots.

"Yeah, he's about as smart as my cat," Short said.

"I thought your cat was dead."

"Exactly," Short said. "But we need someone who can help us

with the traps. Tell Skyler what to do, and he'll happily do it. Like a big obedient dog."

"If *he* wanted to get into someone's pants," Haskins said. "I'd probably volunteer."

"Let's stay on task here," Short said. "After we've completed this first mission, then you can think about all the fun things that giant dummy might do with you."

The night before they had put everything into motion, Haskins called Short to express, one more time, some of her concerns.

"I have to tell you," Haskins said in a whisper, like someone else might be listening to the phone call. "I'm still more than a little nervous about all of this."

"We'll be fine, Maddy," Short said. "If someone does get in trouble for this, it will be Skyler and the Prez. They're the ones who will be setting the traps."

The two women chatted for a few more minutes, and they said they would see each other at the meeting place in the morning. Then Haskins said, "Just know I'm more than a little nervous about all of this."

Before they'd recruited Loots and Nixon, Short and Haskins had followed two men they knew to be trappers. Haskins knew from her travels with her father where a fur buyer lived in Ellensburg. The man had a shop behind his house, and she had seen her dad go in there a few times. Her dad always smelled of Marlboros, but when he returned to the car after being in the fur buyer's shop, he carried the scent of death with him. It made her stomach turn.

Short and Haskins watched the place for two weeks. Several men came and went, but there were two who seemed to be regulars, bringing in animal hides every four or five days.

"Those are the men we want," Short said when they saw the men show up one afternoon, one after the other. "They are obviously successful and are checking their traps often."

Over the next week, Short and Haskins shadowed the men, one at a time. Finally, they were able to carefully follow each to a spot in the mountains where they got out of their rigs, put on packs, pulled some small traps out of their trucks, and headed up a trail.

Short marked the spots on a GPS unit, and the two women went to work recruiting Loots and Nixon to help set the traps that would eventually, hopefully, catch the trappers and stop them from killing the innocent animals that died either in the traps or by the trappers' hands.

Finding Nixon and Loots was easier than Short and Haskins thought it might be. They posted some cryptic messages on several Facebook pages that seemed to be frequented by ASPCA members and other animal lovers, as well as a few dating sites that catered to dog and cat fanatics.

Haskins was probably right about the Prez, Short thought, as he had answered one of the ambiguous messages on a dating site almost immediately. Short didn't care. She sent him a private message and got the feeling that he would be willing to participate in whatever they had cooking.

Loots had been recruited by Haskins. She'd sat next to him in a 100-level biology class, the big guy's second go around in the course, and for some reason he liked her looks. She had helped him with some homework and soon enough she had talked him into coming along and helping out.

"I don't think he really comprehends what we are doing," Haskins said of Loots after he'd agreed to join the group.

"That's okay," Short had said. "He's the perfect person to pack those bear traps up the mountain and help set them."

When they met up at Short's apartment after setting the traps and learning that the two targeted trappers were headed up the trails, there was a palpable energy in the room. Short and Nixon were noticeably excited, Haskins was worried, and Loots, well, he was Loots.

"Do you think we are going to catch any bears in those traps?" Loots asked.

"Are you serious?" Nixon asked.

"Well, yeah," Loots said. "They are bear traps, right? And there are bears up there where we put them."

"I guess it's possible," Haskins said sympathetically.

"If we get one, what are we going to do with it?" Loots asked. "I don't think catching a bear by the leg is going to kill it."

"Let's cross that bridge when we come to it," Short said.

Loots leaned over to Haskins and said, "I don't remember crossing any bridge."

"I'm worried that one or both of those men might not be able to get out of the traps if they get caught in them," Haskins said. "If it stays snowing up there like it was when we drove out of the mountains, they could be in real trouble."

"That's the point, isn't it?" Nixon said. "If the word gets out that trappers are being trapped, others might think twice about continuing."

"The word can get out without someone dying," Haskins said.

"Aren't you the one who hated trapping the most?" Nixon asked. "What's done is done. Not much we can do about it now."

"We could hike up and check on them," Haskins said. "You'd go up there with me to check on the traps, wouldn't you, Skyler?"

"Yeah, but I'd want a gun," Loots said. "A bear would be pretty pissed off with his leg in that big steel trap. I wouldn't want a bear coming at me unless I had a rifle."

Nixon just shook his head.

"Listen," Short said. "We're getting ahead of ourselves. We don't even know if either of those guys got caught."

CHAPTER 4

When Steve Reid came to, he had two inches of snow covering his hat, coat, and pants. He was shivering, both from the cold and the pain in his leg. It was on fire, and that's when he remembered the predicament he was in.

He tried again to pull the jaws of the bear trap apart with his hands, but he couldn't move them even an inch. He looked around again for a small log or a heavy branch that he could use as a pry bar, but as he scanned the area, he could see the snow was even deeper than before.

"Let's think," he said to himself.

He had his pack, which carried his pistol, a big bottle of water, several granola bars, and some waterproof matches. Reid was adept at starting fires, in all weather conditions, but to do so would require that he be able to move around and find the necessary materials.

If he could drag the trap to the pine tree that held the other end of the chain, he might be able to find enough dry pine duff by digging under the snow to get a fire going. But bigger, dry branches and logs would be needed to build a fire large enough to keep him warm and dry. And he would need even more to sustain it.

Reid was a mile up the creek and had been following a little-used game trail. The chances of some random person walking up the trail were miniscule. There was a slight chance that an elk hunter might stumble across him, but over the years he had been running this line, he had only seen one hunter this far up the creek. No, if he was going to get out of this predicament, he was going to have to do it himself.

He had marked each of his trap settings on a mapping application on his phone. The satellite image of the area showed where the traps were set, marked by a red X. The app was loaded onto his phone at home where he had access to the internet, but it worked anywhere in the mountains even without cell service. That did him little good in trying to contact anyone for help, however. If he had copied the map for his wife, she would at least know where to send authorities if or when he failed to get home. But he hadn't.

Moving at sloth-like speed, Reid held the trap with both hands and pulled it, and his ensnared leg, off the ground to make a small step. Again, a stabbing pain shot up his leg, but he ignored it and completed the step. Another deep breath, and he completed the next step. He looked up and estimated he was maybe three or four more agonizing steps from the pine tree. Encouraged, he slowly worked the trap closer.

When Reid finally reached the tree, he was exhausted. He was in very good physical shape from hiking through the mountains regularly, but the two yards he had just traversed with the bear trap on his broken leg took almost everything out of him. There was a constant pain in his leg, and every inch of the short walk had made it even more intense.

The green branches of the pine tree were thick all the way to its twenty-foot top. They weren't thick enough to stop the heavy snow from piling up around the trunk, but it was better than sitting out in the open. Green branches and dead branches bent down to the ground and created a modest canopy. It took some effort, but Reid slowly maneuvered around and under the low branches and then sat with his back against the pine tree.

After resting for a few minutes, Reid started thinking about the stories of the mom who found the unbelievable strength to lift a tipped refrigerator off her child, or the man who was able to pick a car up high enough to save his buddy pinned underneath it. If they could do that, he thought, he could pull the jaws of the trap off his leg.

He sat up, worked his way up onto his good leg, positioned the trap into a spot where he felt he could get the best angle on the device, and grabbed a jaw in each hand. Then, with all his strength, he started pulling the two sides apart.

One inch, two inches, three inches they separated, and just as Reid was about to get the two sides four inches apart, his left hand slipped and the trap snapped back.

"ARRRRRGHH!" he screamed.

Reid fell back against the tree and let the pain subside.

After sitting there for a while, he looked at his watch. Because he wasn't precisely sure what time it had been when he'd stepped in the trap, he had to guess, but it was now 3:50 in the afternoon. He believed he'd been in the trap for just over an hour.

After sitting, resting, and assessing the situation, Reid again got busy. It was going to be dark in an hour. If he was going to make it through the night, he needed to build a fire, and somehow, he needed to get enough fuel to keep it going. And he had to find the fuel in a six-foot radius of the pine tree.

With his hands and his good left leg and foot, he started pushing snow away. He pushed and scuffled and dug, and within a couple minutes he had uncovered a three-inch layer of pine needles, along with several pine cones. The needles on top of the layer were wet from the snow, but there was a layer underneath that was mostly dry. It was a good start.

Reid grabbed up as many handfuls of the dried needles as he could reach and piled them next to him at the base of the pine tree. Then he gradually moved to the left and repeated the process. Within twenty minutes, working his way around the tree while pulling the chain and trap with him as he moved, he had seven good piles of dry pine needles and cones.

Next, he surveyed the branches in the pine tree, as well as the branches in a fir tree that looked to be just close enough to reach. There were several branches that looked dead in the pine tree and should be dry enough to burn. There were even more in the fir tree.

Every time Reid moved, the trap on his leg moved and sent another shockwave of pain through his body. Still, he knew he had to have fire to survive, and that kept him going. If he could just collect enough dry wood to get him through the next few hours, he believed he could make it to morning without getting hypothermia.

Reaching up into the tree to break off a dead branch a foot over his head was a chore. The ones two feet over his head were almost impossible. Slowly, trying to move without creating any more pain than there already was in his leg, he broke nine branches out of the bottom of the pine tree that would burn.

Next, Reid focused on the fir tree. Dragging the trap on his leg with the heavy chain attached through the snow that was now ten inches deep, he inched his way to the tree. When he was halfway to the fir tree, he moved the chain until it got hung up on something under the snow. The chain stopped with a thud and pulled on the trap.

"Awwww," Reid screamed again out of frustration and pain.

He reached down, grabbed the chain, and tried to lift it off whatever it was stuck on. The chain didn't move, so Reid worked back to the spot where it was snagged and reached into the snow. Following the chain with his hands into the snow revealed that it had snagged up on a small log. Reid grabbed the log, lifted, and to his surprise it broke free. The log felt wet but not waterlogged. Maybe it would burn. It was a struggle, but Reid pulled the log back to his spot under the pine tree, left it with the piles of pine needles and dead branches, and moved again to the fir tree.

Getting the dead branches he could reach out of the Douglas fir took more effort and time. When Reid was moving the eight branches back to the pine tree, he noticed it was starting to get dark. He looked at his watch. It was almost five o'clock. Had he really been working for an hour to gather the wood?

As he looked around, he also noticed that the snow was finally letting up. It wasn't stopping but it was no longer the complete whiteout it had been for most of the past three hours. That gave him a glimmer of hope.

When he was situated back at the pine tree with his fire materials around him, he pulled his pack around and found the matches. He made a small pile of pine needles and broke some smaller twigs off the fir branches he had collected and placed them on the pile. Then he lit a match and watched as the needles took off like they were soaked in kerosene.

Within two minutes, Reid had a small, crackling fire going. He knew he would need to manage it to not use up his wood too quickly. He wrestled the big log over next to the fire in hopes that the heat would dry the outer portions enough that he could get it to burn.

That done, he pulled the tube from the top of his pack that led to a water bladder and took a good, long drink. As he was drinking, he remembered he had a first aid kit in his pack that contained some ibuprofen. He grabbed the pill bottle out of the kit, opened it, shook out three of the tablets, and gulped them down with another drink. He doubted it would help much, but even a little relief from the pain would be welcomed.

Next, Reid ate two of his four granola bars. He thought about only eating just one, or half of one, but decided that given his situation, starvation was going to be low on the list of what might kill him, so there wasn't much sense in rationing them. If he didn't get off the mountain in the next twenty-four hours, he was probably going to freeze to death anyway.

The fire comforted him somewhat, so he lay back and took in the warmth. As Reid watched the small flames flicker and listened to them sizzle as snowflakes hit the embers, he again tried to figure out how he was going to get his leg out of the trap. He remembered reading about a hiker in Utah who, a few years before, had had the courage and fortitude to cut his own arm off to save his life when it became wedged in between some rocks. As Reid remembered it, the guy used the weight of the rock to break the bones in his arm, and then sawed the arm off with his pocket knife. With the arm removed, the hiker used the rubber tubing from his water system to create a tourniquet to stop the bleeding.

Reid wasn't sure, but he thought at least one bone in his leg was broken. He had a knife and he had the rubber tubing—everything he needed to get out of the trap. But could he do it? He needed to think about that. He wasn't in that dire of a situation, he thought. At least, not yet.

The warmth of the fire hitting his face felt good. The pain reliever seemed to be helping. Reid laid his head against his pack, closed his eyes, and fell asleep.

CHAPTER 5

Maddy Haskins had slept in fits and spurts through the night. The snowstorm that was pounding the Cascades had worked its way to the southeast and had started dumping on the Kittitas Valley around nightfall. As she watched the snow falling in the pole light across the street from her apartment in Ellensburg, all she could think about was the two trappers up in the mountains. If they had stepped in the bear traps, chances are they were stuck out in the storm and were cold, wet, and possibly injured.

She had no idea if they had been successful in trapping the two men. At first blush, she really liked Short's plan. The idea of trapping a trapper so they could feel what the poor animals that ended up in traps felt was perfect.

What neither of the women knew at the time was Washington State's trapping regulations had made leghold traps illegal, and now the trappers were all using live-catch, cage-style traps. If an animal that was not being targeted ended up in one of the traps, they were released unharmed.

Haskins was awakened by a nightmare. In the dream she was walking with the other members of their little group and suddenly, a trap snapped around her leg. Instead of helping her get out of the trap, the others turned and ran back down the trail, leaving her in the cold and snow.

The fear of being alone in the cold, dark woods startled her awake. She was covered in sweat, and her left leg had somehow become so wrapped up in the sheet, she could barely move it.

Now, fully awake, she worked her foot out of the sheet and went to the window to see if it was still snowing. It had stopped at some point, but looking at the vehicles in the apartment's parking lot, she saw most of the cars were covered in six inches of snow. Maybe more.

Thinking about it, she believed there must be twice that much snow in the higher elevations of the mountains where they had set their traps. If one or both men were trapped, what were the chances they could get out of the huge traps? If they couldn't, how long could they survive?

Short said she was sure the authorities would never be able to figure out who had set the traps unless one of the team members— and now Haskins was thinking of Loots—said something to someone. If they were caught, they'd surely be arrested, but from the little research Haskins had done, they probably would do little or no prison time.

If, however, one of the men were to die because they were caught in one of their traps, and the sheriff, or whoever, figured out they were the ones who'd placed them in the woods, each member of their group could, and probably would, be charged with murder.

"I'm not so sure of that," Short had said a few days earlier when Haskins had presented that very scenario. "I think we're free of that charge. The Prez and Loots would probably be charged, though, because they were the ones who actually set the traps."

Haskins, in the wee hours of the morning, looking at all the freshly fallen snow, now wasn't too sure Short knew what the hell she was talking about. Didn't Charles Manson go to prison for life for sending his minions to kill Sharon Tate and those other people in California? He was nowhere near the murder scene, yet because he coerced his followers to commit the crime, he was charged and sentenced right along with them.

She looked at the clock next to her bed. It was five minutes to five o'clock. She knew what she needed to do.

Haskins jumped into the shower to get rid of the bed sweat, climbed into her hiking clothes, and called Loots.

"Hullow," Loots said after finally answering the third time she tried his cell phone. The two previous times she'd called, it rang and rang and then went to voicemail.

"Skyler, I need your help," Haskins said. "You need to get up and get dressed."

"Who is this?" the big man asked in a slow, sleepy voice.

"It's Maddy. We need to hike up and check on those traps. I'm worried one or both men might die if we don't."

"Geez, really?" Loots said. "It's pretty snowy out there."

"That's why we need to go. We need to take your Jeep and go check on them."

"Okay. When do you want to go?"

"Now. As quickly as we can."

"It's still dark," Loots said.

"By the time we get up to the trail, it will be light. Can you please get dressed and come pick me up?"

"I guess. What if there is a bear in one of the traps?"

"They're all hibernating. We don't need to worry about bears. What we need to worry about is if one of those men were to die. We'd be in some serious trouble."

"How can they die? Their foot would be in the trap. That wouldn't kill anyone."

"They might freeze to death if they have to stay out in the woods for too long. Just come get me. Bring your cold weather gear and be prepared to hike in the snow."

"Okay," Loots said. "Give me twenty minutes."

"Okay," Haskins said. "Do you have a tire iron in your Jeep?"

"Yeah, why?"

"Because we are going to need something to pry those traps open if we've caught one of the men. And bring plenty of water and something to eat. Who knows how long we might be up there if the snow is deep."

Loots said he would bring water, food, matches, and would check to make sure he had a tire iron. "I'll see you in twenty minutes," he said.

Twenty-five minutes later, a purple Jeep CJ-5 pulled up in front of the lobby door at Haskins' apartment house. She quickly walked out to the rig, opened the passenger door, and climbed in. The Jeep was jacked up and had huge tires, making it difficult for anyone under seven feet tall to get into it.

"You should supply a ladder to your passengers so they can get in," Haskins said after she struggled to get into her seat.

She looked and saw a big white bag on the center console next to Loots. A red Jack in the Box logo was on the bag.

"Sorry I'm late. I stopped to get us some food for the road. Hope you like croissants." He pronounced croissants as "croy-saints." "I bought six of the breakfast croy-saints and thought you'd like one."

"That's very thoughtful of you," Haskins said. She was actually kind of hungry and grabbed the bag of food and dug out a sandwich. "Want me to unwrap one for you?"

"Yes, please," Loots said.

Haskins ate two of the croissants as they drove and was surprised she was hungry enough for a second one. Loots gobbled up the other four.

"You normally eat that many breakfast sandwiches?" she asked after he finished the last one.

"No, I usually don't eat any breakfast, but I thought if we were going to be hiking up there in that deep snow, we might need a little extra fuel in the tank."

Maybe the big lug wasn't all that dumb after all, Haskins thought.

"I'm hoping that when we get up there, both their trucks will be gone, which would mean they either didn't get caught in the traps or they were able to get out of them and down to their rigs."

"Did you tell Melissa we were doing this?" Loots asked as they worked their way up through fourteen inches of freshly fallen snow on the Forest Service road where one of the trapper's trucks had been parked at the trail.

"No. She would have tried to talk me out of it."

"I thought you wanted someone to end up in the traps," Loots said.

"I did. But the more I thought about it, what with all the snow that was falling, someone could die, and I don't want to go to prison for the rest of my life."

"Melissa said that wouldn't happen because we couldn't be caught," Loots said.

"Yes, she did. But it still could happen. So that's why we're going to go check on them. Thanks for coming along."

"I don't want to go to prison either," Loots said with a worried look on his face.

They drove to the spot where a silver Chevy Silverado used by one of the trappers had been parked. But when they got there, it was gone. Haskins looked at the snow and saw there was no sign that the truck had driven out in the past few hours.

"Are you sure this is the spot?" Loots asked.

Haskins, who had both trappers' vehicles marked on an onX app on her phone, looked at the screen one more time. They had arrived at the red X that had been used to mark the truck on the GPS unit.

"Yep, this is where that Anderson guy had his trapline. Do you recognize walking up that creek?"

"The snow makes it look different, but yes, I think this is it."

"So," Haskins said, "that means Anderson made it out and is presumably home safe and sound. Let's head to the second truck."

It took a half hour of navigating the snowy Forest Service roads, and as they were getting to the next X on her phone, Haskins said, "It's just around this next bend in the road."

Loots slowly maneuvered the Jeep around the bend, and as soon as he saw the snow-covered vehicle parked in a wide spot in the road just ahead of them, he stopped.

"Shit," Haskins said. "This is marked as Steve Reid's trapline on the GPS. He's still up there."

Loots parked the Jeep behind Reid's truck, a dark gray Toyota Tacoma, and turned the engine off.

"How far up the trail did you leave the trap?" Haskins asked.

"I don't know," Loots said. "The Prez marked it on his phone. I just remember we walked for a while until we found one of the cage traps stuck into some brush against a tree."

"Ok, let's grab the packs and get going. If Reid is in the trap, he should be easy to find."

Loots pulled a tire iron out of the back of the Jeep, threw his pack on his back, and started walking.

Haskins literally jumped out of the Jeep and hurried along to follow.

"You're going to have to walk a bit slower for me," she said after they'd walked a hundred yards. She had already fallen ten yards behind the big man. "Your stride is twice as long as mine, plus the snow is deeper on my shorter legs."

"Okay," Loots said. "I just want to find this guy and get out of here before we get into trouble."

CHAPTER 6

It was still snowing hard when Luke went to bed. He'd had a long day checking on elk hunters and was dead tired. He had talked to Jessie Meyers at seven o'clock, and she still had not heard from her son Austin.

"I'm sure he's fine," Luke had said, again trying to reassure Jessie. "He's well-equipped to spend a night or two in the woods."

"I know I'm probably worrying needlessly, but with all this snow . . ." she trailed off. "And what if he's hurt?"

"I promise if you don't hear from him tomorrow, Jack and I will go look for him," Luke said.

As he lay there trying to go to sleep, Luke thought about his conversation with Jessie.

"What's wrong?" Luke's wife Sara finally asked from her side of the bed. "You're doing a lot of fidgeting."

"I'm worried about Austin," Luke said. "I didn't want to say anything to Jessie, but being gone two days is not good. Especially with this big snow hitting the mountains."

Luke and Sara had been married for five years. She was a strikingly beautiful woman, tall and fit, with black hair and black eyes. From day one Luke believed Sara was about three levels above his league. And she was the smartest person he knew.

Sara was a special agent with the FBI and had been stationed in Yakima to work mainly with the Yakama Indian Nation. Luke had met Sara in an investigation that involved some murdered women whose bodies were discovered in the Cascades.

"You told her you would go look for him tomorrow," Sara said. "What more can you do?"

"Not much, and I may not even be able to do that. I know what's coming in the morning. There will be calls from stranded hunters, and from wives or other family members who are worried about their loved ones possibly stuck in the mountains. It is going to be crazy."

"Can't the Sheriff's Search and Rescue deal with that?" Sara asked.

"I'm guessing they'll be getting the bulk of the calls, but we'll get roped in. I tried to get some of those hunters to break camp and get out of the mountains before this storm hit, but most of those guys are pretty stubborn."

Luke got out of bed and walked over to look out the window. It was still snowing hard, and it was probably worse in the higher elevations.

"There's not much you can do about that now," Sara said. "Come to bed and try to get some sleep. You're probably going to need it."

*

Luke had been awake for an hour when his phone rang at six o'clock. He checked the caller ID and saw it was his boss, Bob Davis, a captain with the Department of Fish and Wildlife.

"Hey, Cap," Luke said.

"Sorry to call so early, Luke," Davis said, "but the sheriff has called and said they are getting calls from several elk hunters up above Rimrock Lake and in the Bumping area. Evidently, they've got a foot and a half of snow up there since yesterday afternoon, and they're calling for help to get out."

"I'll be happy to help however I can," Luke said. "But my guess is nothing short of a Bradley tank is going to be able to pull them out if they're stuck in that deep of snow."

"Sounds like some are just planning on abandoning their camps and vehicles for now," Davis said. "They're going to try walking out but would like to be picked up if there is any way."

"Yakima sheriff's deputies and Search and Rescue have access to snow machines," Luke said. "That seems like a more prudent way to go."

"They're planning on using the ones they have. But from the number of calls already coming in this morning, we're going to need all hands on deck. I'm going to call Hargraves and Peterson next. After I talk to the sheriff again, I'll let you know where to go."

"About that, Cap," Luke said. "I've had several calls from my neighbor. Her son Austin is hunting up in the Taneum and hasn't been in touch for two days. He was supposed to be home night before last because he had classes at YVC yesterday. She's really worried."

"That's the young man you've been mentoring the past few years?" Davis asked.

"Yes, you met him a couple times when I brought him by the office. Anyway, I told her I would do what I could to look for him. I know his rig and kind of where he might be hunting, so if you could work it so that is where you send me, I would appreciate it."

"Consider it done," Davis said. "Kittitas Sheriff's Office hasn't called for help yet, but I'm guessing I'll be hearing from them soon enough."

"Thanks, Cap. I'm going to head that way now and will stay in touch."

"Good luck," Davis said and clicked off.

Sara had gotten up when Luke did and fixed him eggs, ham, and pancakes. They always shared the cooking duties, and their breakfasts were normally very simple—yogurt, fruit, maybe cereal and toast, but this morning Sara was in full country breakfast mode.

"You're going to need the extra calories," Sara said as she shoveled another pancake on Luke's plate. "And you better take some extra energy bars for Jack. If you get into deep snow, he'll have to work extra hard."

Jack was a constant companion of Luke's before he met Sara, and now, even though the yellow dog went out on patrol with Luke most of the time, he loved being with Sara too. Luke thought about leaving Jack at home, but he liked the idea of having a dog that could help find someone with his nose.

"Energy bars are already in my pack," Luke said.

"You have your snowshoes?" Sara asked.

"Yes."

"How about your inReach?"

"Yep, got it."

The inReach was an amazing little device that, when paired with a cell phone, would allow the user to text anywhere in the world via satellite. No phone service was needed.

Sara wasn't a worrier, but more than once she had mentioned something that Luke would have forgotten if she hadn't, so she always tried to help out.

"How about your freeze-dried food?"

"Got it, thanks," Luke said.

She didn't ask about gloves and a hat. Luke always had extras of those in his truck. Along with other survival gear.

Sara watched as Luke, followed by Jack, headed out the front door to his truck. Luke started the rig, tossed his pack into the back seat, and pushed the snow off the hood and windshield with a shop broom. A few minutes later, they were back in the house, Jack covered in snow and Luke standing on a throw rug next to the door stomping his boots.

"It's going to be deep up there," Luke said as he rubbed his hands together to get some warmth back into them.

"You guys be safe," Sara said, handing Luke a steaming travel mug of hot cocoa. She brushed the snow off Jack and gave Luke a kiss on the lips. "Stay in touch."

"I will," Luke said, then turned to Jack and said, "Let's go, boy."

They hustled out the door, climbed in the truck, and headed down the road.

∗

The I-82 freeway between Yakima and Ellensburg was closed due to a number of spinouts and stuck vehicles, so Luke took the old highway that followed the Yakima River. He got on I-90 at Ellensburg and headed west, but the big digital signs over the freeway told him that Snoqualmie Pass was also closed due to the heavy snow and related accidents. Officials were stopping all vehicles at Cle Elum.

Luke just needed to get a few miles up past Cle Elum, so he pulled up to talk to the state patrol officer who was directing traffic off the interstate there. He showed the officer his badge and told him he was not trying to get over the pass but was heading into the mountains to help stranded hunters.

The patrolman looked at the badge and thought about it for a minute, then waved Luke through. To look official and not tick off the other motorists who were parked along the shoulder, waiting to get up the road, Luke put his blue flashing lights on and moved up the freeway.

He was just about to the exit that would feed him into the mountains when his radio burped.

"Wildlife 148, what's your location?"

Luke grabbed the mic and thumbed the button to talk.

"I'm just heading up into the Taneum."

"We have a call from a woman who says her husband runs a trapline up there, and she hasn't heard from him in twenty-four hours. He was supposed to be home by dinnertime last night."

"Did she give a location for the trapline?"

"She knows it's in the Taneum, but other than that she has no clue. Evidently, trappers keep their trapline locations to themselves."

Luke thought about that for a second. Why wouldn't he tell his wife where the trapline was? It's not like she was going to go out and give the location to some other trapper.

"Okay, get me a name and description of his vehicle."

"Name is Steven Reid. Fifty-two years old. Drives a late-model, dark gray Toyota Tacoma. She says it's a two- or three-year-old truck but didn't know the year."

The dispatcher gave him Reid's phone number and the truck's license plate number, then signed off.

Luke wondered how many other calls he would get like this one. Although he figured most would be lost or stranded hunters. Trappers were pretty savvy outdoors people and could deal with most anything Mother Nature threw at them. So the call about the overdue trapper surprised him. He thought about the call and the man. He hoped he wasn't hurt and kept driving up the snow-covered Forest Service road.

CHAPTER 7

Steve Reid had suffered through a long, miserable night. But when the snow stopped falling in the middle of the night and sometime later he started noticing the black night turning lighter with the coming day, he knew he was going to make it, at least for a while longer.

He had burned up all the small branches he had collected, and he'd even burned his wooden snowshoes. The log he had scrounged up continued to put out at least a little heat as the embers burned away from the inside out.

Every time he moved, his leg would remind him about his predicament. He had taken another three ibuprofen sometime in the night, and it had helped dull the pain slightly. Covering his upper body, his face, and head with his raincoat had helped keep him somewhat dry, and he had slept in short spurts. Still, he was exhausted.

Reid thought about his situation. The idea of cutting his foot off at the spot where the trap held his leg was still not appealing in any way. Several times he'd considered it and then thought he would rather be dead than have to go around in a wheelchair or on crutches the rest of his life.

The hiker who had cut his arm off ended up with a prosthetic arm, and in the magazine interview Reid had read, he was quite happy to be alive and found the new arm worked surprisingly well. Reid had a friend who had lost a foot due to complications with diabetes, and the man walked around just fine, most people never knowing he was using a fake leg. Still, the idea of cutting his own foot off, well, he didn't think he could do it.

As the time ticked slowly by, Reid decided to set some goals for himself. It was seven-fifteen when he checked his watch, and he told himself that at eight o'clock he would eat one of his remaining energy bars.

At eight o'clock he ate the energy bar and set a goal to make it to eight-thirty, when he would take another three ibuprofen.

In between those times, he searched his surroundings and tried to come up with something, anything, that he could burn or use to pry the trap off his leg.

*

As they slowly hiked up the creek bottom, Haskins and Loots talked about their situation.

"I've been thinking about this," Haskins said. "If there is a guy in the trap, we have to help him, but he'll never believe we were just out here and stumbled onto him. He'll know we had something to do with setting the trap."

"That would mean he'll turn us in to the cops," Loots said.

"I'm sure he will," Haskins said. "Maybe not at first, but soon enough. He'll be happy we rescued him, but sooner or later he'll be pissed at what we did."

"We could get him out of the trap and then knock him on the head," Loots said. "Then, when he wakes up, we'd be long gone, but he could get down to his truck."

Haskins thought about that for a minute. How would Loots know how hard to hit a man to knock him out without killing him?

"Too risky," she said. "We could accidentally kill him, and then we'd really be in deep shit."

"If we did kill him," Loots said, "no one would find him for what, weeks, months? By then he would be nothing but bones, and no one would know we were involved."

"Let's not talk about killing him," Haskins said. "That's why we're here now, to make sure he doesn't die."

"If he isn't caught in the trap," Loots said, "maybe he has a cabin up here somewhere and was waiting for the storm to pass. Or maybe he had a heart attack, or fell and broke his leg."

"Let's get to the trap and see," Haskins said. "Any idea how much farther?"

"It's a ways," Loots said. "It took us an hour to get back to the truck after we set the trap, and that was downhill in packed snow. We've only been walking for what, forty-five minutes?"

They trudged on, and as they did Haskins kept thinking. She would see what the situation was when they got to the trap, but an idea was formulating.

*

Melissa Short was worried. And at the same time she was mad. She'd been trying to reach Haskins since before eight that morning and she couldn't get an answer. Finally, she bundled up, cleared the snow off her Subaru, and drove over to Haskins' apartment.

Haskins' Subaru was in its normal parking spot, covered in snow, but when Short went into the complex and knocked on Haskins' door, no one answered. She thought about it for a minute, pulled out her phone, and called Loots. His phone went straight to voicemail.

Then she tried Nixon's phone.

"What's up?" Nixon asked after a couple of rings.

"I'm trying to find Maddy. Have you seen her?"

"I'm still in bed," Nixon said.

"Did she call you?" Short asked.

"No. Haven't seen her since we left your place last night. Are you sure she's not still asleep? You know how she is. I've talked to her in the afternoon, and she'd just woken up."

"I'm at her apartment now, and she's not answering her phone or the door."

"Maybe she has those noise-canceling things in," Nixon said. "I think she wears them so she doesn't have to listen to those idiots in 4-B partying all night."

"Maybe," Short said. "But I'm worried with all that talk last night about going up to see if either of our traps caught anything."

"You mean, *anyone*?"

"Yeah, whatever. I think she could get Skyler to do pretty much anything she asked. And if she wanted to go up there, he would take her."

"I doubt anyone would go up there in this snow. Besides, I heard on the TV that Snoqualmie Pass is closed and they aren't letting anyone go up the freeway past Cle Elum."

"Skyler has that truck with the big tires," Short said. "I bet he could get up there."

"It's a Jeep," Nixon corrected. "And yeah, it could probably go in some pretty deep snow."

"If you see or hear from her, let me know, would you?"

"Sure thing, boss," Nixon said. "I'm going back to sleep for another couple hours."

"Don't you have class?" Short asked.

"They've canceled all the classes today because of the snowstorm."

"Of course they did," Short said and hung up.

She'd grown up in Montana, where nothing short of a full-on blizzard with temperatures twenty degrees below zero would close schools. A large percentage of the kids at the university walked to class. Why they couldn't walk to class in the snow made no sense to her. Whatever. That meant she didn't have to go listen to the boring drone of the professor in her Latin music appreciation class.

Not being able to talk to Haskins worried her. She thought the Prez could be right, that Haskins had found out classes had been canceled and had gone back to sleep with her earbuds in, but that didn't feel right. Short wanted to go see if Skyler's big-tired Jeep was parked at the house he shared with about nine other guys, but since she had never been to the house, she had no idea where to look.

She couldn't think of anything else to do, so she drove back to her apartment and tried to reach Haskins one more time on her phone.

*

"Are your feet wet?" Haskins asked Loots as they walked slowly up the hill.

"No, are yours?"

"Yeah, and it pisses me off because these boots were expensive, and they are guaranteed to be waterproof."

Loots looked down at her boots and said, "Your boots are probably fine. I think the snow is so high, it is getting up your pantlegs and on the tops of your socks, and the water is wicking down into your boot. That happened to me one time."

"Crap. My legs are so cold I can't tell if they're wet too."

"Not much you can do about it now," Loots said. "You could walk back to the Jeep and turn the heater on. I'll keep going to see what we got going on at the trap."

She thought about that for a minute. A heater in the rig sounded pretty good. But she just wasn't sure what Loots might do or say if he found a person in the bear trap.

"Naw, I'm good," Haskins said. "We should be getting there soon, right?"

"I'm not positive, but yeah, we have to be getting closer."

They walked in silence for another ten minutes, and Haskins said, "I have an idea."

"Okay," Loots said. "Whatcha got?"

She went on to tell him that she had a friend in high school who had an old cabin near Cle Elum. She hadn't been there in years, but following the friend on Facebook, she had learned the girl's father was terminally ill with some kind of cancer. Haskins had called and talked to the friend, and the conversation turned to the fun times they'd had at the cabin during several summers.

"That was fun," the friend said. "Sadly, since Dad got sick, we haven't been there in two years."

"So, what I was thinking," Haskins said to Loots, "is, if there is a guy in the trap, we get him down to your Jeep, get some duct tape around his hands and feet, take him to that cabin, and hold him there."

"Can you get into the cabin?" Loots asked.

"Yeah, I remember where they hid the key. My guess is it's still there."

"What about neighbors?"

"There aren't any. The cabin is set back in the trees. No one can see it from the road."

"I guess we could do that, but what good would it do? Why not just let him go?"

"He'll figure out we're the ones who set the trap," Haskins said. "And he'll turn us in. He might not know our names, but he'll be able to describe us. They'd probably do that thing where they get an artist to draw our pictures and pass them all over the place. And he would know your Jeep. That purple color makes it stand out in a whole parade of Jeeps."

"It's not purple," Loots said. "It's grape."

"What do you think?" she asked.

"I don't know," Loots said. "This is getting kind of complicated. It's making my head hurt."

"Well, we can't just leave the guy in a trap because he will die. If we can get him someplace where he won't freeze to death, then we can talk with Melissa and see if she has any ideas."

"Okay," Loots said. "But we don't even know if we have caught anyone yet."

"We should know soon," Haskins said as she looked down at her feet. "Damn boots."

CHAPTER 8

The snow was deeper in the mountains. Luke figured it was twenty or twenty-two inches deep in some places. He had the Chevy in four-wheel drive, low gear, and it was doing okay, but a couple times on steeper inclines he really had to push it.

He hit a flat spot and was contemplating chaining up when he looked up and saw two snowmobiles coming down the road. The drivers of the snow machines, all bundled up and wearing helmets with tinted face shields, pulled up next to Luke's truck and turned their machines off.

The driver of the lead sled tipped his face shield up and said, "Don't think I'd go much farther, officer. The snow is deeper, and there is a pretty steep hill about a half mile up the road. You could get down it, but not back up is my guess."

"I was just thinking about chaining up," Luke said. "That wouldn't help?"

"Oh, probably," the first driver said after thinking about it for a few seconds. "But there's not much sense in going any farther. We've been five miles up the road this morning and haven't seen a living thing."

"No abandoned rigs?" Luke asked.

The second sled driver was shaking his head, and the first driver said, "Not that we saw."

Luke could see they weren't hunters, so he asked, "What brings you up this way?"

"We love to ride in fresh snow," the first driver said. "Plus, since it's elk season, we thought there might be some stranded hunters up here after the big snowfall. Hate to see someone in a bad situation."

Luke could see the men were both in their sixties, probably retired, and were enjoying not having to work. He handed the lead sled driver his card.

"I'm kind of doing the same thing," Luke said. "We're getting calls from concerned family members who haven't heard from their elk hunter relatives. And I'm looking for one particular vehicle. It's a white Ford F-250 with a gray canopy on the back. You haven't seen it have you?"

Both riders thought about it, and then the first driver said, "No, sorry."

"If you see it, would you mind giving me or my office a call?" Luke asked.

"There's about a million white Ford pickups out there," the second driver said. "I have one myself. But not many with gray canopies."

"We'll look around," the first sled driver said.

Luke thanked them and watched as they dropped their face shields, started their snow machines, gave a quick wave, and buzzed off down the road.

After the snowmobilers were gone, Luke sat and thought about it for another minute. This was the area where he thought he might find Austin Meyers. The two had talked before the elk season, and Austin had said they were seeing some elk up off this road. He wasn't exactly sure where Austin and his buddy might be camped, but he hoped it would be on this road within a few miles. If the snowmobilers hadn't seen any rigs up the road, there wasn't much reason to go any farther.

He once again thought about putting the chains on and then figured if he had made it this far without them, he should be able to make it back. Luke put the truck into gear and started moving up the road to find a place to turn around when his radio came to life.

"Wildlife 148?"

"Wildlife 148, go ahead."

"Kittitas County Sheriff's Office had a call they wanted us to know about."

"Okay, go ahead."

"A man called in to say he found a bear trap up in the Taneum yesterday. It was set in the trail next to one of his marten traps, and he was concerned that someone was purposely setting them to catch hikers."

Luke immediately thought of the call he'd had from the woman whose trapper husband had not made it home for dinner and had been gone all night.

"Roger that," Luke said. "Give me his name and phone number. I'll call him as soon as I can get cell service."

The dispatcher gave Luke the information, and he scribbled it down on his notepad and signed off.

"That's not good," Luke said to himself.

In the back, Jack's tail wagged, thumping the seat.

"Hey, boy. Nice to have you awake back there. Maybe we should hop out and get a little fresh air."

He knew Jack was probably ready to pee and, as he thought about it, he was too. He stopped the truck, left the engine running, climbed out, put his heavy coat on, and let Jack out of the back. The big yellow dog hit the ground and took a few bounds. The snow was up to his stomach.

"Good thing we're not walking very far in this stuff," Luke said to Jack as he watched the dog jump and jump and jump through the deep snow.

They both relieved themselves, and Jack did a perimeter search of about a fifty-yard radius. In short order he tired of trying to navigate the deep snow and bounded back to the truck where Luke opened the back door. The big dog jumped in.

"Well, that was refreshing," Luke said to Jack as he reached into his pack for energy bars for him and the dog.

As they ate their bars, Jack gobbling his up in a matter of seconds, Luke thought about what to do next. He wanted to talk to the trapper who'd found the bear trap, but he also felt he should keep working the roads to see if he could find Austin or any other stranded hunter who might be out there.

The call to the man who'd found the bear trap could wait. He needed to keep checking the roads in the area, so Luke turned his pickup around and headed down to where he could grab a different Forest Service road.

*

Three different times, Steve Reid unsheathed his hunting knife, pulled his pantleg up, and put the blade to his entrapped leg. As a medic, he had seen the Army doctors perform emergency amputations before, although he had never performed one. He knew how to cut his own leg off, and where, but he just had to make himself do it. He'd been trying to work up the courage to make the first cut, but each time he stopped and put the knife away.

Reid had heard about coyotes that, when stuck in a leghold trap, would actually gnaw their leg off to escape. He'd trapped many coyotes but had never seen it in person. But now, faced with what was possibly going to be the same life-and-death decision, he knew what the coyotes must have been going through.

Just because he was tired of sitting in the same position for such a long period of time, Reid had picked up the chain and trap, along with his leg, and had hobbled to another position under the tree. His fire now was nothing more than some smoldering embers, and he was starting to shiver. In the night, after the snow stopped falling, he had pulled his down vest out of his pack and put it on. But now, with no fire to help stave off the freezing temperatures, he was starting to shake uncontrollably.

These were the first signs of hypothermia, he knew. According to accounts from others who had suffered from hypothermia, after the violent shivers, a sense of warmth would set in, and that is when most people fell asleep and basically froze to death.

Thinking about all that spurred him on. He stood and for the umpteenth time scanned all around for something he might be able to use to pry open the trap. Then it hit him. What about his marten trap? It wasn't very big, but folded down, the all-metal trap might just give him the leverage he would need to pry the bear trap open. It was worth a try.

He moved too quickly when he thought of the trap sitting ten feet away, and his leg screamed at him for making such a stupid move.

He stood frozen for a few seconds, letting the pain subside, and then, carefully, he again picked up the chain, and his foot with the giant trap clamped to it, and moved inch-by-inch toward the marten trap. The chain around the tree stopped his progress short of the trap. He thought if he could lie down, he should be able to reach it, but when he tried, the thing was eight inches out of his reach.

Reid squirmed this way, then that, trying to somehow get another few inches closer to the trap. Every move made the broken bone in his leg throb. As hard as he tried, he couldn't quite reach the wire trap.

He carefully worked his way to his feet again and looked around. He needed something he could use to reach out and hook the trap and drag it to him. A green branch on the pine tree would work, which meant he had to slowly work his way back to the tree. The movement was making his broken leg hurt more than it had in hours, but it was also moving some blood through his body, stifling the hypothermia, at least for the time being.

Reaching the tree, Reid pulled his knife from the sheath one more time and used it to cut a sturdy, five-foot branch.

"This will do," he muttered to himself as he whittled the smaller branches off the main branch he had just cut.

When he had the branch cut down, with one of the bigger secondary branches cut so it formed a hook, Reid again hobbled through the snow and lay down as close to the steel cage trap as he could. He reached his hooked branch out to the trap and pulled on it just far enough so he could grab it with his hand. The small trap was tethered to a stake in the ground so it couldn't be carried away by a coyote or another scavenger. By pulling with all the strength he had left, Reid was able to yank the stake free.

As he lay there, exhausted, hoping the metal trap would be the key to his escape from the bear trap, he thought he heard a woman's voice. In his current condition, his mind could be playing tricks on him, so he listened more intently. It was most likely a bird, or a squirrel coming out to check on the snow. But it could be a human. Please be a human, he thought to himself.

Then, there it was again. Definitely a woman's voice.

"HEY!" Reid yelled weakly. "HELP! PLEASE HELP!"

He heard footsteps coming through the brush.

"Thank God," Reid said as he buried his face in his hands. "Thank God."

CHAPTER 9

Travis Carter found the little cabin high in the Cascades the day before the big storm hit. He was looking for something as a hideaway, and the cabin was perfect.

The white Chevy pickup he was driving was stolen from a used car lot in Eagle, Idaho. One of the lazy salesmen at the car lot had left the keys to the truck tucked up on the visor over the steering wheel, and Carter had taken the opportunity to make the truck his own. No down payment. No credit checks. No proof of insurance. One minute the truck was sitting on the car lot, and the next it was his, and he was out of there.

It had taken Carter all of twenty minutes to switch plates with a similar white Chevrolet pickup sitting in a tavern parking lot in nearby Meridian, and driving carefully not to speed getting out of town, he hit I-84 heading north and got the hell out of there.

He hadn't planned on shooting anyone. It just kind of happened. Carter had been in this particular liquor store in Boise off and on for a month and saw just what kind of business the store was doing. Lots of the transactions were in cash. He noticed that the sales clerk would clear his cash drawer and put the money in a slot—which Carter believed was connected to a safe—at one minute to eight o'clock each night. It didn't matter if the clerk was in the middle of a sale; he would stop, clear almost all the cash from the drawer, and then return to helping the customer. Each time he did it, he would turn and show the cash to a small camera that poked out of the wall behind the register and then stick the money in the slot.

Carter had no idea how much cash was being stuffed into the safe each evening, but to a guy who never had more than twenty bucks in his pocket at one time, it looked like a million dollars. If he could get a bunch of money like that, he could finally get out from under his old man's roof.

His father had been nothing but an asshole to Carter his whole life. He didn't beat him with his fists, but he was constantly on the boy, who could never seem to do anything right.

Carter got bad grades in grade school, and by the seventh grade he was smoking pot with his buddies. He wasn't all that smart to start with, and the pot just made him stupider. He got caught shoplifting a time or two and was getting in fights in high school. When he got kicked out of school, his old man pretty much disowned him.

Yes, he'd let Carter come back and stay in his old room when he found out his son had gotten a job as a janitor at the hospital in Boise, but the free room and board came with a heaping helping of guilt. The old man was always chirping at Carter for one thing or another.

When he lost his job at the hospital, he didn't tell his father. Besides, he never should have been fired in the first place, Carter thought. Every janitor in the place was stealing pills from the pharmacy in the basement. He was the one who just happened to get caught.

His plan to rob the liquor store was formulated over a few

weeks. He had waited for the perfect time to pull it off. And tonight was it. With his old man's .38 revolver stuck in his pants under a black, zip-up sweatshirt, Carter tugged a blue and orange Boise State ballcap down low on his forehead and walked into the store. He was looking at the booze on a shelf near the cash register while keeping an eye on the clock and the clerk. As he stood there perusing the selection of fine sipping whiskeys a little before eight o'clock, Carter double-checked and saw there was no one else in the store.

Everything was a go, and at two minutes to eight, he stepped up with a bottle of Knob Creek Single Barrel Reserve, plopped it on the counter, and waited as the cashier held up a finger, pressed a couple buttons on the cash register, and started pulling a wad of hundreds and fifties out from under the main money tray. Then the clerk grabbed a stack of twenties and tens from the top of the tray, put all the bills together, and started to turn to the camera.

"Stop right there," Carter said and poked the .38 Special in the cashier's face.

The man stopped, and Carter said, "Hand it over."

Carter hadn't considered the possibility that the cashier might also be packing a handgun, but as the man handed the cash across to Carter with one hand, he started pulling a pistol out from under his shirt with the other.

Luckily, Carter saw it coming, and as he was grabbing the cash with his left hand, he shot the clerk in the chest. Not hesitating for a second, Carter turned and ran out of the store, down the sidewalk, and into the alley where he had parked an old, ten-speed bicycle.

As he rode the bike, he took the Broncos ballcap off, pulled a white stocking cap out of his sweatshirt pocket, put it on, and stripped the black sweatshirt off to reveal a red and black checkered flannel shirt. He tossed the sweatshirt and ballcap into a dumpster at the back of a restaurant as he rode by and kept peddling for the Albertson's grocery store four blocks away where he'd parked his old man's Chrysler Sebring earlier that evening.

Amazingly, his plan worked. The liquor store manager, who

was on the other end of the camera behind the cash register, watched it all happen. He called 911 immediately and described Carter to the cops, but it was like the shooter had disappeared into thin air.

One old lady, who was walking a pair of Pekingese dogs named Bert and Ernie, had seen a man riding a bicycle come out of the alley near the liquor store around the time of the robbery. She said the guy on the bike was wearing one of those red and black checkered shirts like hunters wear and had on a white stocking cap.

"We go out for our walk precisely at seven forty-five," the woman told the police officer who saw her walking the dogs near the liquor store. "Bert needs to do his business at eight, or we'll have a mess on the carpet, so I make sure we are out and down the sidewalk so he has a place to pass his bowels. I wear my poop glove, I call it a poop glove, and with my scooper I always pick up when Bert is done."

"Yes, ma'am," the officer said. He was going to thank her, but she kept right on talking.

"Now, Ernie, he is not regular at all. He might ask to go out at seven in the morning or three in the afternoon. Sometimes he'll go two times a day. I'll tell you, officer, these two sure keep me on my toes."

After complimenting the little lady on what he thought might be two of the ugliest dogs he'd ever seen, the officer thanked her and went looking for any other possible witnesses.

When Carter got to the Albertsons, he took the time to park the bike next to a small tree, locked it to the tree's trunk with a bike lock—as if someone was actually going to return for it—and walked over to the Sebring. He really wanted to pull the wad of cash out of his pocket to count it but resisted the urge.

His next stop was the used car lot in Eagle. A couple years before, he had taken a well-used, older Corvette for a test drive and noticed the salesmen had placed the keys on the visor when they were done with the drive. Carter couldn't afford even a high-mileage, abused Corvette, but he had always wanted to drive one and decided to give this one a spin.

He had driven by the car lot earlier in the day and saw they had a white Chevy 1500 pickup for sale. Knowing there were approximately twenty-seven thousand of that make, model, and color of truck on the road just around Boise, he thought it would work fine for his purposes.

The car lot closed at seven, but he had driven by in the afternoon, parked across the street, and watched the two sales guys at their desks for a few minutes. When they became engrossed in something on their computer screens, probably video games, Carter snuck across the street, opened the truck's door, and took the keys.

His old man was going to be pissed that Carter had taken the Chrysler and used it to knock off a liquor store, but he would get the car back and maybe he would get over it. Carter thought about that for a little longer and decided that, no, the old man would never get over this one. Oh well, he was never going back to that shitty part of his life again anyway. Whether he had needed it or not, he'd been browbeaten enough.

Carter's plan was to go to Alaska. He didn't know that much about the huge state to the north but figured that as big as it was, a man could get lost up there. He hadn't quite worked out how he was going to get there. He knew there was a highway that went through Canada all the way to Alaska, but since he didn't have a vehicle when he first was planning everything, he wasn't sure if he would drive there or not.

His immediate goal was to get to Seattle. If the cash from the liquor store was enough, he would buy a plane ticket to Fairbanks or Anchorage, and then he could go somewhere and just disappear. If there wasn't enough money from the liquor store, well, he was sure he could find a job for a while in Seattle.

As it turned out, the liquor store cash added up to thirteen hundred and seventy-three dollars. He spent a little of it when he stopped for gas twice, and on one of the stops for fuel he grabbed a Whopper with cheese, fries, and a strawberry milkshake at a Burger

King that was open all night in one of those giant truck stops that had magically popped up along the freeway.

After the meal, he started getting sleepy, so he pulled into a rest stop and stretched out on the seat for a while. He was awakened three hours later by the morning sun boring into his eyelids.

As he merged onto the freeway from the rest stop, he set his sights on Seattle. A few minutes later, he turned the radio on to try to find some good old country music. He wanted some Hank, or Waylan, or Willie, not that pop rock crap the so-called country music stars were putting out these days.

Carter was running through the dial when he came across George Jones singing "He Stopped Loving Her Today" and thought, finally. After Jones's last nasally note faded, the news came on, and an announcer with a very serious voice said, "State police are looking for a man who was involved in a shooting and liquor store robbery in Boise last night. The perpetrator shot the store cashier and got away with nearly ten thousand dollars in cash."

"Well, that's bullshit," Carter said to the radio.

Then it dawned on him. Someone was scamming the insurance company to make a tidy little post-robbery profit off his holdup.

The announcer went on: "Police believe the gunman is twenty-nine-year-old Travis Carter from Boise. He is five foot ten inches tall, one hundred and sixty-five pounds, with short reddish-brown hair. Carter is believed to be traveling in a silver 2008 Chrysler Sebring. Police think he could be traveling north through Oregon and are asking people to call 911 if they see the car, as Carter is believed to be armed and dangerous."

How did they figure out who he was so quickly? At least they didn't know about the pickup.

The announcer continued: "The liquor store cashier, a forty-two-year-old Max Ormlan from Meridian, Idaho, was rushed to Saint Alphonsus Regional Medical Center in Boise after receiving one shot from a handgun to the chest. Mr. Ormlan unfortunately died from his gunshot wound."

A moment later, a different voice, this one of a man who

seemed much happier, said: "Next up, we've got some Okie from Muskogee coming your way!"

Carter heard Merle Haggard singing, but he didn't pay attention. He was too busy thinking about what he needed to do next. He had killed that guy in the liquor store. The cops were going to be looking hard for him.

He thought about the money and said, "Ten thousand dollars, I wish." Then he pushed the Chevy up the freeway. Washington was just a hundred and fourteen miles away according to the last freeway sign.

*

Carter stayed on I-84 up through Oregon, crossed over the Columbia River into Washington on I-82, and continued north and west. He stopped for gas and a Carl's Jr. double cheeseburger at another giant truck stop in Prosser, got back on the interstate, and kept driving.

He had passed by two different state patrol cars in Oregon and had seen one in Washington so far. None even gave him a second look. He also had seen about two hundred white Chevy pickups like the one he was driving. Still, he needed to be watching.

As he drove, he was looking directly at the Cascade Mountains in the distance. Carter could see a wall of gray clouds that seemed to be enveloping the mountains. It looked like he was going to be driving directly into one hell of a storm.

He continued to listen to various radio stations as he drove, not caring now if it was good country music or bad. What he wanted to hear was any news about what the police might be doing in their search for him. Three different stations were warning of an impending snowstorm for the Cascade Mountains, where up to three feet of snow might be falling in the higher elevations.

"If you are planning on driving over the mountain passes this evening, please be prepared for heavy snow," one of the radio announcers said.

Finally, Carter heard something about the robbery in Boise. A female newsperson on an all-talk AM station was reading a story about the shooting and robbery.

The newsgirl said, "Authorities now believe Travis Carter is driving a white 2014 Chevrolet 1500 four-wheel-drive pickup. They believe he is headed north through Oregon, as police found security camera footage of him at a truck stop in LaGrande, Oregon."

The report didn't say how the cops figured out he was in the pickup, but they must have found his old man's car not far from the used car lot where he'd stolen the pickup.

As he drove past Yakima, to Ellensburg and on toward Seattle, two things worried him. He was headed into a major snowstorm. And he now was a killer. The cops were looking for him in the white truck he was driving. He needed to do something. He needed to get someplace where he could think. And what he really needed most was some sleep.

Carter's gut told him to get off the freeway, so at an exit past Cle Elum, he dropped off the freeway and got on a siding road. From there he headed up into the mountains, taking what looked to be a well-used Forest Service road. There was compact snow on the roads from an earlier snowfall as he got higher in elevation, but he put the truck into four-wheel drive and kept going.

He grabbed a spur road off the main road, continued to climb, and took another spur road. He was looking for cabins. Back in the mountains of Idaho, summer cabins were everywhere. If he could find a cabin around here that wasn't being used, he could break in and stay a while, until the heat was off.

Unfortunately, there were no cabins around. Or at least none he could see. Carter decided to turn around and pulled into what looked like a driveway. He caught just the outline of a roof of a building in the trees, so he pulled in farther.

Up the two-track drive, sitting just as pretty as you please in the pristine snow, sat his hideaway.

He was surprised the cabin was unlocked, and even more surprised when he found a nice cache of canned food on the shelves and firewood already split and ready for the fireplace.

Carter started a small fire, opened a can of Stagg chili, stuck the can next to the fire to heat it up, and watched out the door as some of the fluffiest snowflakes he had ever seen started floating out of the sky. It looked like someone had plucked a hundred white geese and dumped a whole truck full of their feathers out of the clouds.

He went back to stir the chili, pulled a bottle of water out of a big case full of them, and watched the fire for a couple minutes. When he went back to look out the door, the snow had turned from fluffy and nice to downright ugly. It was now snowing so hard he could hardly see the white truck parked thirty feet away.

As he ate the chili out of the can, he watched the snowfall. He had been in snow many times in Idaho, but this was like something he had never seen before. It started to scare him. Fearing the probability of getting snowed in for who knew how long with the snow piling up as fast as it was, Carter threw the can of unfinished chili into a snowbank, jumped into the Chevy, and headed back down the mountain.

He found a mom-and-pop motel in Cle Elum, signed in under a fake name, and paid cash for a single room for the night.

"You are lucky, Mr. Johnson," said an older woman with gray hair streaked with green and blue dye. "That was our last single room. We'll be sold out within the hour on doubles, what with the big snowstorm on Snoqualmie."

"I'm glad you had a room," Carter said. "What time is checkout?"

"Eleven o'clock," the woman said as she handed him the key for the room.

"By the way, I like your hair," Carter said.

"Seahawks colors," the woman said. "I'm a big fan."

"Well, good luck to them this weekend," Carter said and walked out the door.

A fat orange cat sat on the windowsill and watched him walk away.

CHAPTER 10

The lower road was easier to maneuver because the snow was not quite as deep. And a vehicle had passed on the road sometime during the morning, so Luke stayed in those tire tracks. He also saw that the two men on the snow machines had been on the road based on the unique track design in the middle of the two tire tracks. Or he thought it was the same men.

Since the snowmobilers were on the road and looking for Austin's pickup, Luke decided he would try another road. He didn't know it at the time, but if he had gone another mile up the road, he would have seen Steve Reid's snow-covered Toyota Tacoma parked on a pullout, with a purple CJ-5 parked behind it. Luke found a good place to turn around, headed back to the main Forest Service road, and moved on to the next spur road.

Up that road a mile or so, Luke ran into two hunters hiking down the road. Both men had backpacks on over bright orange coats, with rifles slung over their shoulders. As he pulled up to the men, Luke saw one of the men was older, maybe in his late fifties or early sixties, and the other man was younger, maybe in his late thirties. They were the same height and had similar features. A father and son, Luke guessed.

He stopped the truck just short of the men and hopped out.

"Hey, guys," Luke said.

"Boy, are we glad to see you," the older of the two men said.

"How's that?" Luke asked.

"We were camped down over the hill," the younger man said, using a hitchhiker's thumb to point back up the road. "Our rig is stuck, and we're out of firewood. We decided to hike out."

Luke got the men's names, Jerry and Jerome Gaines, father and son.

"My mom's probably freaking out," the younger Gaines said. "We were supposed to drive out and call her every day, just to let her know we were doing okay. Dad has some heart issues, and she has it in her mind he's going to tip over out here someplace."

The older Gaines laughed. "All I do is wander over to my favorite stump and sit there all day," Jerry said. "I'd have a better chance of tipping over mowing the lawn at home."

Luke laughed and asked, "Any luck on the hunt?"

"Naw," Jerome said. "I saw a good bunch of cows, with two spikes in the herd on opening day, but they were running through the trees so fast it was impossible to get a shot."

"I had one big five-point come by me and stand there like that one on the insurance TV commercials," Jerry said. "But, of course, I don't have special permit for that one."

"So, what was your plan?" Luke asked.

"The plan was to walk until we found someone, such as yourself, to give us a lift down to where we can get some cell service and give the wife a call to come get us," Jerry said. "We'll come get the rest of the stuff when the weather allows."

"Which might be next spring," Jerome said.

"Are there any more camps up this road?" Luke asked.

"There were, but a couple different motorhomes and guys with travel trailers got out of here when they heard the snow was coming," Jerome said. "I saw a pickup parked in the trees with a small tent next to it about a half-mile past our camp. I don't know if they're still in there or not."

"What did the truck look like?" Luke asked.

"Let's see," the younger Gaines said as he thought about it. "It was white, I think, but had a different color canopy on the back."

"Gray canopy?"

"Yeah, come to think of it, it was gray. Didn't match the truck at all."

"Was it a Ford, do you remember?"

"Could've been," Jerome said. "But I really wasn't paying attention. And that was three days ago. I'm thinking they got out of here when the snow started."

"I'm looking for a friend in a white Ford with a gray canopy. He was supposed to be home two days ago. You didn't see anyone around the truck or tent, did you?"

"No, it was pretty quiet," Jerome said. "No fire going or anything."

"What day was this?"

"Let's see, today is Tuesday, so that must have been on Saturday."

"Okay," Luke said. "Load your gear into my truck. Don't mind my dog. He's friendly and will be glad to see a new face or two. He looks at me about twelve hours a day. I'll give you a ride down the mountain."

"Sounds great," the older Gaines said as he was pulling his backpack off.

"Does your mother text?" Luke asked Jerome Gaines.

"Yes, but we always had to drive down a ways to get any service to call or text."

"I have one of these satellite texting devices," Luke said, pointing to his red inReach Mini unit clipped to his shirt. "I can text from anywhere in the world from my phone with this."

"That's pretty cool," Jerome said. "How much are they?"

"About three hundred bucks," Luke said. "And then you have a monthly service fee, but in a situation like this, it is well worth it."

Luke got the cell number for Jerry Gaines's wife and texted: *Mrs. Gaines, this is officer Luke McCain with the Department of Wildlife. I have your husband and son with me and we are coming down out of the mountains. Everyone is fine. Their truck got stuck in the snow and they needed a ride. Can you start heading toward Cle Elum. I'm going to take them there. They will call as soon as there is cell service.*

A few moments later, Luke checked his messages. The return text read: *Thank you so much, I will head that way now.*

"Mrs. Gaines is on her way," Luke said.

"Did she sound freaked?" Jerome asked.

Luke laughed. "I'm sure she is happy to know you are both just fine."

They chatted as they drove, and Luke found out the men were from Moses Lake and had hunted up in this same area for years.

"Some years we get an elk, but most of the time we don't," Jerome Gaines said. "It is one of the fun things we do each year, just Dad and me."

"I don't remember seeing such a big snowfall in one day and night," Jerry Gaines said. "Must've been some kind of record."

"We knew the storm was coming," the younger Gaines said. "But we never thought it would be this crazy. A couple days before the storm, all the elk just seemed to disappear. Like they knew what was coming."

"Mother Nature definitely has a way," Luke said. "You pay attention to the animals and the birds, and you will see they somehow know when there is a big weather change coming."

"I'm guessing we aren't the only ones who got stuck in this deep snow," Jerry said.

"We started getting calls early this morning from hunters who were stuck, and from family members who were worried about their hunters. All our people, plus the Sheriff's Search and Rescue teams are out helping folks."

Luke drove as quickly as the conditions allowed getting down to Cle Elum. He wanted to drop the two hunters off and get back up to check on the truck Jerome Gaines had seen. It sounded like Austin Meyers' truck, and if it was still there, he needed to try to figure out where Austin was.

When they got into cell service, the elder Gaines called his wife, and Luke could hear him reassuring her that he and Jerome were just fine.

Luke took the time to call Captain Davis.

"Hey, Cap," Luke said when Davis answered.

"How's it going, Luke?"

"Okay. I'm hauling a couple stranded hunters down to Cle Elum. One of them may have seen Austin Meyers' pickup, so as soon as I drop them off, I'll be heading back up there. I may need some help and will text you if I do."

"Sounds good," Davis said.

"How's it going otherwise?" Luke asked.

"Pretty crazy. Lots of calls about missing hunters. We have to hope that most are just stranded and that Search and Rescue will find them as they work the roads in the high country."

"Any word on that trapper?" Luke asked.

"Nothing that I've heard. The Kittitas sheriff was going to call me if the guy showed up."

"Okay, well, I'll keep an eye out for his truck, but it sounds like the road where Austin's truck was last seen had very few vehicles on it. Most bugged out before the snow hit."

"Keep in touch if you can," Davis said. "And be safe."

Luke clicked off and said to the men as he pulled into Cle Elum, "I'll drop you off at the Dairy Queen. That way you can get something to eat."

"Sounds good," Jerry Gaines said. "We'd be glad to buy you a burger as thanks for hauling us out."

Luke really didn't want to take the time, but he was getting hungry, so he took them up on the offer.

"I'll just grab a burger and go," Luke said. "Thank you."

On the way back out of town, Luke again had to talk his way through a roadblock, this one on the on-ramp to I-90. The state patrol officer, a woman, looked at Luke's badge. She then saw Jack standing with his feet on the center console.

"Nice-looking dog there," the officer said.

"He's the ultimate chowhound," Luke said, lifting the Dairy Queen bag. "He sleeps in the back all morning, but the second there's food around, he's up and at 'em."

"Where can I get a gig like that?" the officer asked. She was all bundled up and wearing an official blue Washington State Patrol cold weather hat with the fuzzy ear flaps pulled down.

"I've been trying to figure that out myself," Luke said.

The officer laughed, told Luke to "travel safe," and waved him through.

As Luke drove back into the mountains, he finished off—with Jack's help—a double cheeseburger, fries, and a chocolate shake, which he had justified having since it might be a while before he would eat again, especially if he were out looking for Austin.

*

When Travis Carter saw the state patrol car blocking the on-ramp to the interstate, he thought they had somehow found out he was in the area and were stopping cars looking for him. His immediate reaction was to do a U-turn right there, but that would just call unwanted attention to him. So he pulled slowly up to an officer all bundled up in a heavy coat and a funky hat with ear flaps and rolled his window down.

"Sorry," the officer said. "Can't let you through. The pass is closed, so we're turning everyone around here."

Carter thought about it a second and said, "Any idea when it might reopen?"

"No, sir. It just depends on the weather."

Carter turned his truck around and then watched in his rearview mirror as the truck that had been right behind him, kind of an ugly brown pickup with some kind of an insignia on the door, pulled up, talked to the officer, and then was waved on through.

He really wanted to get back up to that cabin. It was the perfect place to stay until the cops stopped looking for him. He couldn't go to Seattle because the freeway was closed, so he would just have to stay at the motel another night—that is if he could get a room again.

Luckily, the woman with the Seahawks-colored hair said they hadn't cleaned his room yet and he could have it again for the night. She would even take ten bucks off the rate because there would be no need for the room to be cleaned. As he headed out the motel office door, with the fat orange cat watching him, Carter asked where the closest grocery store was and got directions to a Safeway just up the road.

He drove to the store, listening to the radio. An announcer came on and said that the National Weather Service had issued a warning that a second major snowstorm with high winds was moving into the Cascades, and the storm was expected to last about twelve hours.

Hopefully, that meant he would be able to get to the cabin tomorrow.

*

It took over an hour to get back to where Luke had picked up the Gaines men. Luke considered putting the chains on, but he decided he would drive up the road until he thought it was getting too deep for four-wheel-drive low gear with no chains. It was a risky move, he knew, but if he didn't have to get out and wrestle the chains onto the tires, it was worth it.

He drove slowly along, watching the Gaines's footprints in the road and slowed when he saw a three-quarter-ton Dodge Ram stuck in a depression just off the road. The truck was tilted so much the driver-side door could not be opened. The men, Luke figured, had had to crawl out the passenger door to exit the truck. The tire tracks led back to a twelve-by-twelve wall tent that looked cold and empty.

According to Jerome Gaines, the pickup truck that might be Austin Meyers' was another half-mile up the road. Luke kept his pickup in low and crept along through the deep snow, paying particular attention to where the road was.

In chatting with the Gaines men on the way down to Cle Elum, Jerry said he'd lost track of the road in the deep snow, and their truck had slid off the road down a three-foot embankment and almost rolled, which had made it impossible to get the truck back on the road. As Luke drove through the heavy blanket of white, he could see how it could happen. The last thing he needed at this point was to do something similar.

He found Austin's snow-covered truck fifteen minutes later. The small, two-man tent that had been pitched nearby was flattened by the snow. There were no human tracks in the deep snow, which told Luke the young men hadn't been here since at least yesterday afternoon.

In the chance that Austin and his buddy had somehow caught a ride back to Yakima with a friend or someone else in the past six hours, Luke fired up his inReach and texted Sara: *Will you please call Jessie Meyers and see if she has heard from Austin today?*

Four minutes later, Sara texted back: *Will do. Stand by.*

Six minutes later: *Still no word from Austin. She is VERY worried.*

Luke replied: *I found his truck, but no sign of him or his friend. Will start looking for him now.*

Sara: *Should I let Jessie know about the truck?*

Luke looked at his GPS and got the coordinates for where the truck was located and replied: *I will leave that up to you. Here are the GPS coordinates if you need to send someone for help.*

Sara: *Send someone now?*

Luke: *Let me look around. I will check in in an hour.*

Sara: *By the way, my weather app says a second wave of snow is headed your way, with high winds predicted.*

Luke: *Great.*

Sara: *B Safe.*

Luke: *Roger that.*

That done, Luke started gearing up to look around. He pulled his pack out, which carried all the necessities for spending two to three nights in the woods, stuffed a puffy coat filled with down into the main compartment, and grabbed his snowshoes.

Jack had jumped out of the truck and was sniffing around Austin's truck. The dog, especially when Luke had been single, had spent as much time at the Meyers' home as he had Luke's. He watched Jack sniff around and thought there was no way the dog would be able to track Austin in this snow. But it was good that he might know their neighbor was around the area.

Luke stepped into his snowshoes, grabbed his hiking poles, whistled for Jack, and started walking up a gradual incline. His idea was to find some high ground where he could search the area with binoculars. What he might see, he didn't know, but it was the best option right now, much better than stumbling around without having a clue about which way to go.

If he was going to find Austin, it sounded like he better do it soon. The idea of a blizzard coming in was going to make it all the more difficult.

Chapter 11

Maddy Haskins thought she heard a man yelling up ahead. She stopped and whispered to Loots, "Listen."

"What?"

"I just heard a man yelling for help."

They were quiet and listened for a minute and then they both heard the man.

"What should we do?" Loots whispered.

"We need to go let him out of the trap. But we need to act like we had no idea how he got in it."

"Okay," Loots said.

They heard the man's voice say again, "Please, help me!"

"We'll just have to figure it out as we go," Haskins said. "I'm guessing he'll need help walking down to the trucks, and when we get him there, we'll have an idea what to do."

"We will?" Loots asked.

They walked up the trail another fifty yards and spotted the man, lying face down in the snow, holding onto a metal cage. His right leg was in the bear trap chained to a pine tree.

"Thank you, thank you," Reid said when he saw the pair coming up the trail. "I had no idea how I was going to get out of this thing."

"What happened?" Haskins said as she hurried up to where Reid lay.

Loots followed Haskins and knelt next to Reid.

"I stepped in this damn trap. I'm pretty sure my leg is broken."

"We can help you get out of it," Haskins said. "Try to find something to pry the trap open, Skyler."

Loots started to look in his pack for the tire iron, and Haskins stopped him. She had been considering the situation, and if they just happened to have a pry bar, it would give Reid an idea they were aware of the trap and the possibility someone was in it.

"I've looked," Reid said. "But this deep snow covers everything, and I can't move very far because of the chain."

"Go look for something," Haskins said to Loots.

The big guy stood up and looked around.

"You're going to have to walk around and see if you can find a sturdy branch or something," she instructed.

Loots walked off, looking at some of the trees in the area.

"I can't believe you came along," Reid said. "No one ever walks up this drainage."

"We saw a truck covered in snow and wondered if someone might have gotten lost or was hurt," Haskins said. "So we decided to take a hike."

Reid was looking at the girl with her big bug glasses and the gold ring in her nose. Haskins could see him trying to process all that.

"I'm sure glad you did," Reid said. "What is your name?"

"My name is Maddy, and that is Skyler," Haskins said with a head-nod in the direction Loots had gone.

"My name is Steve. I've been in this trap for almost twenty hours."

"Wow," Haskins said. "How did you make it through the night?"

"I was able to build a fire. But I burned up all the wood I could collect, including my snowshoes, and probably wouldn't have made it through another night unless I did something drastic."

"Well, we'll get you out of here just as quick as we can."

Reid was still just staring at Haskins. She could see that he was trying to figure out how someone who looked like her would take off into knee-deep snow in search of a ghost.

"Do you need water?" she asked. "Or something to eat?"

"No, I'm good," Reid said, looking away and closing his eyes. "I just need this damned trap off my leg."

Haskins watched the man, who looked very tired. She could see he was shivering.

Three minutes later, Loots came tromping down the hill with a bent, rusty, steel fence post in his hands.

"I tripped on some barbed wire and thought it might be attached to something, so I pulled on it," Loots explained. "Came up with this post."

"That will work!" Reid said as he sat up, hope in his face.

Haskins stood back and watched as Reid instructed Loots where to place the end of the fencepost inside the jaws of the trap.

"My leg is impaled on one of the teeth of the trap, so it will have to come off it before I can pull my foot out."

Loots got behind Reid and started pushing the fencepost away from them, working it as a lever to pry the trap apart. The jaws of the trap slowly separated, and when it was far enough apart, Reid said, "Just hold it right there. Mandy, can you pull my leg away from the tooth on the one side?"

Haskins ignored that he'd called her by the wrong name and reached down and started to grab the leg from the inside of the trap.

"No!" Reid barked. "Come from behind and push it. If the trap were to spring back, your hands would be crushed."

She hesitated for a moment, thinking about getting her hands caught in the trap, and then came from behind and slowly pushed Reid's leg off the tooth. As she did, he let out some whimpers of pain.

When it was free, Reid grabbed the freed leg with his hands and pulled it out of the trap. Loots then let the jaws come back together.

"Thank God," Reid said. "And thank you guys so much. You literally saved my life."

Reid tried to stand up and fell back into the snow.

"Damn," he muttered. "Leg's been in that trap so long, it's pretty much useless."

"Maybe we can make a crutch for you," Haskins said. "And we can help you down to your truck."

She turned back to Loots and said, "Skyler, go find a sturdy branch or small log about five feet long."

Loots obediently turned and walked back up the drainage.

"Can you bring me my pack?" Reid said to Haskins, pointing back to the pine tree with the chain around it. "I have a small hatchet in there. It will come in handy cutting the crutch to the right size."

"Here you go, Mr. Reid," Haskins said after she walked over and grabbed the pack. "It's heavy. Whatcha got in there?"

Reid thought about it for a second. Had he told the girl his last name? He was ninety-nine percent sure he hadn't. And if he hadn't, they already knew who he was, which meant they knew about the trap.

"Just some trapping supplies, first aid kit, and matches," Reid said. "Saved my life."

He had his .45 caliber Berretta in the pack, and now he was glad it was close at hand.

"Speaking of a first aid kit," he said as he reached in for the small pack that held bandages and antiseptic cream. "Do you mind doctoring that wound on my leg?"

"No, let me help you," Haskins said.

Reid handed her a large bandage, some alcohol swabs, and the ointment and pulled his pantleg up. The wound was not big, but it looked bad because the skin all around it was purple with bruising. Half his leg was one big contusion.

"That doesn't look good," Haskins said with an ugly face.

"Don't want it to get infected," Reid said.

As Haskins worked on getting the wound cleaned and dressed, Reid watched her work. He had seen a thousand hikers over his years in the woods, and this girl looked nothing like any he had ever seen before.

"You do a lot of hiking?" Reid asked Haskins as she was applying the bandage.

"No," Haskins said. "In fact, I'm not really a hiker at all. But Skyler has this Jeep with big, huge tires, and when the snow hit, he thought it would be fun to come up into the mountains to drive in it. We saw that Toyota down on the road all covered in snow and worried that someone might be lost or hurt. So we took a walk up this way."

"Long way to walk just on a whim," Reid said.

"That's what I told Skyler. He's like seven feet tall and takes giant steps. I asked if we could turn around three times, but he wanted to keep hiking. He thought it was fun hiking in this deep snow."

Reid looked at her with skepticism.

"My feet are all wet because the snow melted up in the legs of my pants and soaked the tops of my socks," Haskins continued. "We were finally going to turn around when we heard you calling."

"Good thing I heard you talking," Reid said. "I was considering cutting my leg off to get out of the trap."

Haskins looked away from the bandage she was applying and into Reid's face. "Seriously?"

"Yep, had my knife out several times. If you hadn't come along, it was going to be my only way of getting out of here alive."

"No. You wouldn't really have done that, would you?" Haskins asked.

"Better than dying."

"Geez," Haskins said. "But how could anyone do that?"

Reid didn't say anything and just let her think about it for a while.

"You know, I've had plenty of time to think about this," Reid said. "And I'm of the opinion that someone set this trap to purposefully catch me." He watched Haskins' face as he said it. Her eyes shot away from his for just a split second, and he knew. She was involved in this somehow.

"Found something," Loots said as he high-stepped through the snow down the hill, carrying a dead lodgepole pine. "I'll need to break a piece off after we figure out what length to make it."

"Mr. Reid has a hatchet," Haskins said to Loots. "We can use that to cut it to the right size."

Reid focused on Loots for the first time. The girl was right. The kid was a giant. And he appeared to be strong and fit. Strong enough to haul that heavy bear trap this far up the creek. Reid was in no kind of shape to take on someone that young and that fit. Even without a hurt leg. He was definitely going to keep his pistol handy.

First things first, though, Reid had to get to his truck. And the couple seemed ready to help him do so. But why would they set a trap for him, just to come up and release him? He'd have to think about that and pay extra attention to everything the two were doing.

CHAPTER 12

The phone rang, and Nixon looked at the caller ID and said, "What now?"

Short said, "I am REALLY getting worried about Maddy. She can't be sleeping this long. I'd bet a hundred bucks she got Skyler to drive her up to check on the traps."

"Is that so bad?" Nixon asked.

"Do you want to go to prison?"

"No, but what's that got to do with Maddy and Skyler checking on the traps?"

"Because if one or both of the trappers are caught in the traps we set, and they let them go, those men will certainly figure out that the traps were set for them and run right to the police. The next thing you know, they'll be at our doors."

"Those men haven't seen us," Nixon said. "So how are they going to find us?"

"If Maddy doesn't squeal, it's a sure bet Skyler will. And he probably won't even know he's doing it."

Nixon laughed.

"I'm serious," Short said. "He'll say something stupid, and we'll all be in it up to our ears."

"We're already in this up to our ears. So, what do you want to do about it?"

"Will you go up there with me?"

"In what?" Nixon asked. "Your Subaru isn't going to make it up there if the snow is deeper than what we have here. And it most certainly is."

"It's four-wheel drive," Short said.

"That doesn't matter. If you're pushing snow with the bumper, it's not going to get very far. Believe me."

"Okay, well, I'm nervous as hell sitting here. I wish she would call."

"You could come over, and we could fool around," Nixon said, then laughed. After a pause, he said, "Just kidding."

Short didn't say anything.

Then he said, "Call me when you hear from Maddy, and if I hear from Skyler, I'll call you."

"Okay," Short said and rang off.

Short thought there was still a chance Maddy and Skyler hadn't gone to check on the traps. If that was the case, then they all would be okay. But right now she had to go on the assumption they had gone to the mountains. She needed to figure out what they were going to do if the men had been caught. Nixon was right. They were already up to their ears in this deal. She needed to be thinking about a plan B and an escape plan.

*

After trying to run ahead, Jack eventually fell in behind Luke and walked in the path that was being created by the snowshoes. Even then, the big dog had to jump at times to stay in the tracks. They trudged through the snow, up a gradual incline, and once they'd gone out of a stand of older fir trees, Luke could see a bald high spot about three hundred yards ahead.

"C'mon, boy," Luke said and kept walking.

The climb to the top of the bald mountain took another fifteen minutes, and when they arrived, Luke was sweating. He knew he shouldn't have pushed it so hard because now he was wet with perspiration and he was probably going to get cold. But he was getting more worried about Austin by the hour, which made him push harder.

The spot on the knob allowed Luke a hundred-and-eighty-degree view of miles of country, most of it in timber, almost all of it covered with the heavy snow. He could see to the west, and the sky was one big wall of dark gray clouds. It was the next storm Sara had mentioned. He had no idea how soon the storm was going to arrive, but Sara had said this storm was coming with some high winds. He believed it would be here sooner rather than later.

Luke pulled his binoculars out of the pouch on his chest, put them to his eyes, and started searching. It was a sea of white, with some green peeking out here and there where gravity had pulled the weight of the snow off some of the evergreen branches. He looked for anything out of the ordinary. A splotch of color or obvious human tracks in the snow. There was nothing.

He was on his second pass, poring over the land below, when something caught his eye. He pulled the binoculars down and looked with his naked eyes. He couldn't see what he'd seen in the binoculars. Luke put the binos to his eyes again and looked more intently. There it was. A small ribbon of gray smoke filtering up through the trees. Luke watched the smoke and tried to see the fire that was creating the gray stream flowing out of the trees, but the snow-covered forest made it impossible.

He pulled out his GPS, turned it on, and waited for the unit to acquire the satellites. When the screen popped up, he zoomed in to see where he was in the world. When he had zoomed in enough, he could see the bald knob on which he sat. Of course, the satellite picture had been taken during the spring or summer, so it was green, but it still helped him figure out where the smoke was originating.

Luke marked his location on the map and then thumbed the screen in the direction of the smoke. When the satellite photo was hovering over where he thought the fire might be that was creating the smoke, he looked for any cabins or roads. He was pretty sure there were no cabins in that area. And if he remembered correctly, there were no roads either. Still, he wanted to check.

According to the GPS, the smoke was roughly two miles from the nearest road. And there were no structures anywhere near where the smoke was coming out of the trees. Luke figured that in the deep snow it would take two hours to get there from where he was.

Someone had started the fire, he thought, but was it Austin? And if it wasn't Austin, was it some other hunter who was stranded?

He pulled his phone out and connected it to the inReach satellite texting device. He checked his coordinates, estimated the coordinates of where he thought the smoke was, and typed both sets of coordinates into a text and sent it to Sara.

Coordinates for where I am and where I am heading. I have spotted smoke. Believe it is Austin. Send help asap.

He waited five minutes, then ten. While he waited, Luke took a good drink of water, and he and Jack ate an energy bar.

The return message from Sara finally arrived.

Got it. Will send help asap. Storm is moving your way fast. Please be careful.

Luke looked to the west. The gray wall of clouds was definitely closer, and he could feel the first touches of a breeze building. Sara might be sending help, but with a blizzard coming in, he believed he would be on his own, at least until the storm blew over.

He thought about heading back to his truck to ride out the storm, but if he could get to the spot where the smoke was coming up before the storm hit, he could build a shelter and hole up there, with Austin or whoever was at the fire.

To be doubly sure which direction he needed to head, Luke

took a reading on the compass on his phone. Even if the GPS didn't work, he figured he could still get to the smoke.

"Let's go, boy," Luke said to Jack as he grabbed his hiking poles and started down the slope.

*

There is no such thing as walking in a straight line when moving through the mountains. Fallen trees, broken terrain, boulders, and other obstacles make walking directly from one point to another impossible.

Besides avoiding the obvious impediments, Luke was constantly zigging and zagging to avoid knocking avalanches of snow off tree limbs on top of him. And even though his snowshoes kept him mostly on top of the snow, he had to be careful of stepping into places where the snow had built up over fallen logs or dips in the ground that might not hold his weight.

It was a slog.

He stopped often to double-check that he hadn't gotten off-course, which he had twice. Everything looked different down in the trees.

When he could see some sky through the trees, Luke looked for the smoke but could never find it again. He had to rely on his GPS, which showed he was basically going in the right direction, and he was getting closer.

The wind that Luke had felt up on the knob was pretty much undetectable down in the trees, but every now and then a gust would blow through the treetops, creating a new storm of already fallen snow.

Luke noticed the day was getting darker even though it was only three o'clock in the afternoon. That meant the new storm had almost arrived.

He put his head down and kept marching, slowly, to the point he had marked on the GPS.

*

The walk down the hill was a slow one. Reid used the handmade crutch the best he could, but the deep snow made it way more difficult than it would have been on dry ground. Every step required him to lift the base of the lodgepole up out of the snow and move it forward. And he was having to keep his bad leg lifted, which was tortuous and exhausting.

"You're doing great," Haskins encouraged as they inched along.

After seeing the difficulties Reid was having navigating the deep snow, Loots offered to pick him up and carry him. Reid told him it would probably make his leg hurt more, and he feared that if the big kid slipped and they fell, it might do more damage to his leg.

As he hobbled along, Reid noticed the sky was getting grayer and darker, which meant more snow was on the way. He didn't say anything about it to Haskins and Loots. They would find out soon enough when the weather changed. He hoped they could get to his truck before the snow started falling.

The wind was starting to pick up too, and twice big gusts blew snow out of the treetops.

"Hope that doesn't keep up," Haskins said with a shiver as she brushed snow from her shoulders.

A few minutes later, off to their left, a huge gust of wind pushed a pine tree, top-heavy with snow, to the ground. The tree groaned and creaked and then came crashing down.

"Geez," Loots said. "I've never seen that happen before. Good thing we weren't under it."

Haskins wanted to run down the hill to the road, but they needed to stay with Reid, who continued to labor walking on one leg with the aid of the crutch.

Farther away, another huge gust pushed a second tree over. They couldn't see it, but they certainly heard it.

"This is getting spooky," Haskins said.

"If you want to, go on ahead," Reid said. "Go ahead and go. I can make it down from here."

Haskins seriously thought about it. Her toes were so cold she could no longer feel them, and with the wind starting to blow and the trees falling, she wanted to be anywhere but here.

"No," she said. "We need to make sure you make it out safely."

They were a half-mile from the road when it started to snow. It was like someone turned on a switch. One minute there was no snow falling, then it was coming down hard. The wind had subsided, but as soon as the snow started, it picked up and started blowing again.

"Holy crap," Loots said to the others. "This is not good."

"What should we do?" Haskins said.

"We're going to get moving," Loots said. He turned, bent down in front of Reid, and pulled him over his shoulders in a fireman's carry.

"No, no," Reid said in a painful cry, but it was too late. Loots had him, and they were now moving at a much faster pace down the hill.

The blowing snow made it difficult to see, but they stayed in their tracks from earlier in the day and kept heading downhill. Luckily, they were moving with the prevailing wind and the snow.

When they arrived at the road twenty minutes later, all three of them were plastered with snow and ice. Loots set Reid down, shook himself off, and walked over to his Jeep. He started the engine, turned the heater to high, put the defrost on, brushed the snow off his windshield, and walked back to help Reid to the vehicles.

"Thank you so much," Reid said. "I can take my truck from here."

He wanted to get away from these two as quickly as he could. He was positive they were involved with setting the trap and he wanted nothing more to do with them.

"You are in no condition to drive," Haskins said. "We'll get you to help. You can come back and get your truck later."

It was time, Reid thought, to get his pistol. He struggled out of his snow-covered backpack, brought it around, reached in, pulled the pistol, and pointed it at Haskins and Loots.

"You don't understand," Reid said. "I am taking my own rig

out of here. I don't know why you set that trap up there, but I know it was you."

With uncanny speed, Loots jumped at him. Reid had only a second to shoot, and just as he pulled the trigger, he was hit so hard it knocked the wind out of him. A second later, Loots hit him in the face with one of his huge fists, and the lights went out.

"That'll hold him for a while," Loots said, looking down at Reid in the snow. "So what do we do now?"

He turned to look at Haskins and couldn't comprehend what he was seeing. She was face down, a slow stream of crimson red oozing from under her body into the white blanket of snow.

CHAPTER 13

L uke could feel the snow before he saw the first flakes. It was cold and wet. Like an invisible atmospheric change all around him. Three minutes later, it was as if he was in a snow globe. It was snowing hard, with a crazy wind circling in the trees, spinning the snow around in all directions.

He had just checked his GPS and knew he must be close to where the smoke had been coming out of the trees. The swirling snow, now coming down hard, was going to make finding the source of the smoke more difficult.

Jack had been on Luke's heels most of the way because the walking was easier in the path the snowshoes were making. Now, though, Luke watched as the big dog moved ahead of him, with his nose held up just slightly. He had seen Jack do this many times over the years.

One time, Luke stopped when he saw Jack doing this very thing, and it probably saved his life because an instant later a wounded black bear charged out of a blackberry bramble at them. Luke, who was armed with a rifle, shot the bear just before it reached him.

Jack had also done the nose-in-the-air thing when he detected a dead cougar in the grass as they were trailing a serial killer in the North Cascades. At the time, Luke hadn't known the cougar was dead, and he suspected Jack didn't either, but he was glad to have had the advance warning.

Now Luke wondered what the dog was smelling. It probably wasn't a bear, as this high up in the Cascades they should all be in dens, but it certainly could be a cougar. Luke hadn't brought along a rifle on the search for Austin, but he did have his service pistol. As he watched Jack turn slightly back and forth, trying to gauge just where the scent was coming from, Luke pulled the pistol.

He had always been a much better shot with a rifle and a shotgun, but if something was close enough, Luke felt like he could do whatever needed to be done with the .45 caliber Glock that was issued to all state Fish and Wildlife officers.

"What is it, boy?" Luke whispered to Jack. He looked in the direction the dog's nose was pointing, but the swirling snow made seeing anything at any distance virtually impossible.

Usually when Jack did this, he would emit a low, rolling growl. Luke stepped closer to the yellow dog to listen. At first, he thought the wind was masking the growl. He listened closely, but there was no growl.

Jack wagged his tail just a couple of times. He took three steps in the direction he was looking and wagged his tail a few more times.

Again, Luke asked, "What is it, boy?"

Then Jack took off bounding in the direction he was looking. Luke looked ahead, but again could see nothing.

"Jack, come!" Luke yelled. All he needed right now was for the dog to get tangled up with a mountain lion.

Jack had been an excellent dog, even as a puppy. He'd been easy to train and could almost read Luke's mind in different situations.

Jack had helped in a number of arrests and had jumped into the fray a time or two when Luke was being physically accosted by ne'er-do-wells. He almost always came when he was called. Almost.

Luke yelled for Jack to come again but watched as the dog struggled through the deep snow, into the trees and out of sight in the heavy snowfall.

There was nothing else to do, Luke thought, but to follow him. His tracks were easy to follow, even with the swirling, stinging snow hitting him in the face. As he walked, Luke listened. Twice more he called for Jack to come, but the yellow dog never appeared.

Luke kept the pistol ready. He didn't know what to expect. Then, when he spotted blood in the snow, he got a sick feeling in his stomach.

"Dang it, Jack," Luke said as he followed the dog's tracks mixed in with the blood.

He trailed the tracks and blood through a thick stand of trees, down into a creek bottom, and up the creek. Finally, through the blowing snow, Luke saw Jack standing there, wagging his tail, next to a person who was waving at him.

"Hi, Luke!" Austin Meyers yelled.

Somewhere along the line, the kid had turned into a man. Now, Luke hardly recognized him. He was pushing six feet tall and wore his dark brown hair short, but not too short. He had a five-day growth of dark stubble on his face, making his big smile of perfectly aligned teeth look even whiter.

"When Jack came running in, I knew you weren't far behind. Boy, am I glad to see you."

"Not as glad as I am to see you," Luke said.

"We have a problem," Austin said. "It's my buddy Jase. He fell and dislocated his ankle. We were going to try to get out of here just when the snow started yesterday, but decided to wait it out. We found this culvert and holed up here."

"What's with the blood in the snow?" Luke asked.

"Jase shot a spike two days ago. We skinned it and cut it into quarters, hung the meat in a tree, and were going to pack them out, and that's when he hurt his ankle. The quarters are a half-mile away or so. This morning when the snow stopped, I went and got a hindquarter and dragged it back here so we'd have some meat to eat. We've been eating freeze-dried meals for the last three days."

"So, how's Jase doing?" Luke asked as he moved toward the culvert.

"We popped his ankle back into place the best we could and have been putting snow on it to keep the swelling down, but I was worried about frostbite. It still hurts really bad, he said, and he can't put any weight on it."

Luke could see that Austin had collected some logs and branches and had built a lean-to type of covering over the front of the culvert that cut under a newly built road. He assumed he had done the same thing on the other end.

"How'd you end up in the culvert?" Luke asked.

"We saw it the day Jase shot his elk, and when he hurt his ankle and it started snowing, we decided to hole up here."

Luke looked above the six-foot, round, metal culvert and saw a logging road had been cut through the area, probably after the last satellite photo had been taken.

"That was good thinking."

"I was going to go grab an elk quarter, hike to the truck, drive to the nearest spot where I had phone service, call for help, and then come back to help Jase. But then the snowstorm hit."

"It looks like we might be here for a little while longer," Luke said. "More snow with these high winds is predicted for the next several hours."

"Geez, our moms must be worried sick," Austin said as he walked to the covering on the culvert.

"They are," Luke said. "I'll text Sara now so she can call your mom and Jase's mom to let them know you're with me. I have Sara working on getting some help here, but this storm may hinder all that."

Luke knew Jase Schlagel from the times he'd been around over at the Meyers' house. Schlagel, who was nineteen, the same age as

Austin, stood just over six feet tall and had dirty blond hair that was cut short on the sides and longer on top. He had bright blue eyes and was lean and fit. The young man looked to be in pain as he lay on some fir bows covered in a couple coats.

"Hey, Jase, how's the ankle?" Luke asked.

"It's been better. Hurts like crazy if I move it at all."

"Have you taken any pain relievers?"

"We don't have any," Austin said.

"The snow has helped numb the pain some and has helped with the swelling, I think."

Luke looked at the ankle, and it was twice the size of what his other one was.

"I have some ibuprofen in my pack," Luke said. "And help is coming as soon as they can navigate this storm."

"We've heard some trees falling with these crazy winds," Austin said. "We're glad we've been in here and not trying to hunker down under a big tree out there somewhere."

Luke took his pack off and started digging for the pain relievers. He also grabbed a roll of sticky tape so they could put together a splint to hold his ankle from moving.

"Here's the ibuprofen," Luke said. "I'm going to go text Sara and let her know what's happening."

"Tell her to tell my mom I'm okay," Jase said. "And let her know I got an elk."

"Will do," Luke said. "Congratulations on that, by the way. I'll check your license and tag later."

Jase chuckled and then stopped, not knowing if Luke was kidding or not.

Jack had wormed his way onto the coats next to Jase, and now the young man was petting the yellow dog.

"Sure glad you found us, Jack," Austin said.

Jack's tail thumped, and he put his head on Jase's thigh. In a second, the tired pooch was sound asleep.

It took a while to get satellite connection on account of the snowfall. But once the little communicator was connected, Luke texted Sara to let her know he had found the boys. He fibbed a bit, telling her that Jase only had a sprained ankle but that both boys were dry and safe. He asked her to keep pushing for someone to come help get Jase out, on snow machines if possible.

Luke: *We have plenty of food and water. Sheltered in a large culvert. Will be fine until help comes.*

Sara answered back: *Good to hear. Stay in touch.*

Luke: *Will do. I will check back in the morning unless something changes here.*

Sara: ♥ ♥ ♥

When he got back in the culvert with the boys, Luke said, "Looks like we are here for the night. They'll send help as soon as the weather breaks. The good thing is we have some fresh elk venison to eat to get us through."

"We ate some earlier," Jase said. "It's pretty good."

"We need to get some more wood to burn," Austin said. "And maybe I should go get another quarter while I can still see the trail."

"I don't think that's a good idea," Luke said. "It's a full-blown blizzard out there and doesn't show any signs of letting up."

"We definitely need some more firewood," Austin said. "I know where we found some earlier, and it's not too far away."

"Okay," Luke said. "I'll go with you. Keep an eye on Jack if you would, Jase."

"Will do," Jase said and stroked Jack's back. "Although I don't think he'd go even if you wanted him to."

Jack didn't even open his eyes.

Luke told Austin to grab his rifle just in case. The young man slung it over his shoulder, pulled on mittens and a wool hat, and they headed out into what Luke thought might be the worst blizzard he had ever experienced.

CHAPTER 14

L oots was paralyzed. He had no idea what to do next. A hundred thoughts were running through his head. The first was to flee. With the snow blowing sideways and piling up fast, he wanted to get out of there and not look back. But he couldn't leave Maddy just lying there dead in the snow. If she was, in fact, dead.

That's what he needed to do, check to see if she was dead. He had been to his grandmother's funeral and had gone up to the coffin at the front of the church and looked at her dead face, but other than that, he'd never seen a dead person before.

On television, the police always felt a person's throat to see if they were dead. He didn't know what they were feeling for, but that's what they did, so he did the same thing. He walked over, knelt next to Haskins' body, and reached for her neck.

"Aaaaack!" Haskins screamed when she felt the cold hands on her throat.

"Ayyyyyy!" Loots screamed and jumped back three feet when Haskins screamed.

He caught his balance and walked back to Haskins, who was now trying to push herself up in the deep snow.

"Help me roll over," she said.

"I thought you were dead," Loots said as he helped her roll over and then sit up.

"Not yet," she said as she slowly worked her hand up to clear snow out from under her big round glasses. "I'm shot though. In the side."

"Oh boy," Loots said, looking at Haskins and the blood in the snow. "This isn't good."

"We need to get to the hospital as quick as we can," Haskins said. Then she looked at Steve Reid lying in the snow.

"Did you kill him?"

"No, I just punched him in the face. Knocked him out."

"We need to get him in the Jeep and take him with us," Haskins groaned.

"What? Why?"

"Because if we don't, he'll either freeze to death out here or he'll wake up and drive down the mountain. Then the police will be after us."

Fighting the wind and snow, Loots helped Haskins to her feet. After she was standing, she unzipped her parka and lifted a heavy sweater to reveal a dime-sized hole in her left side just above her waist.

"Oh boy," Loots said again after looking at the bullet hole, which was still seeping blood.

Haskins turned a little and said, "My back is burning. Can you see what it is?"

Loots moved in closer and said, "Yes. It's another bullet hole. Did he shoot you twice?"

"No," she groaned. "I think the bullet went all the way through my body."

"Oh boy," Loots said one more time. He couldn't believe how

calm she was about the whole thing. He would have been screaming like a four-year-old.

Haskins had Loots help her to the Jeep and then sent him back to Reid.

"Grab his backpack, put the pistol in it, and bring it here," Haskins said. "Then pick him up and get him into the back seat. You have any duct tape?"

Loots did as he was told, and within a few minutes he had the still-unconscious Reid in the back of the Jeep, with his hands and feet bound in silver tape.

As Loots was carrying Reid to the truck, Haskins pawed through Reid's pack, found the first aid kit, and pulled out some gauze and tape. She put the gauze on the front bullet hole, wrapped the tape around her midriff, put a second wad of gauze on the hole in her back, and then wrapped the tape around her body a couple more times.

When Haskins was loaded in the Jeep, Loots did a U-turn to head down the mountain. As he drove, the wind buffeting the Jeep and the driving snow made it almost impossible to see the road. He turned his windshield wipers on to high, but they weren't doing any good. The snow wasn't sticking to the glass, and the wipers couldn't reach out and clear the view ahead of the Jeep in what was now a full-blown blizzard.

Loots looked over at Haskins, who was leaning against the door with her eyes closed.

"This isn't good," he said.

"What isn't good?" she asked without moving.

"It's snowing harder. I can't see a thing."

"Well, take it slowly," Haskins said. "But we can't stop. I need to get to the hospital."

*

Reid regained consciousness just as Loots and Haskins were discussing the snow. His face hurt, his ribs hurt, and his leg really hurt. He was happy to hear they were headed for medical help, but then he realized his hands and feet were wrapped up in duct tape. He remembered pulling the trigger on his pistol but didn't know he had hit the woman until she was talking about needing to get to the hospital.

"What are you going to do with me?" Reid asked wearily.

"We're taking you to the hospital," Haskins lied.

"Why did you set that bear trap up there? Was it to catch me? Why would you do that?"

Neither the big man driving nor the woman replied.

Reid watched as Loots drove the Jeep very slowly down the road. It was a full-on blizzard outside the vehicle, the likes of which he had never seen before. If he had been driving, he would have found a place to pull off the road and wait the storm out. It couldn't snow and blow like this for too long.

"This is very dangerous," Reid finally said. "Run off the road and get stuck, and then we'll never get to the hospital."

Haskins just groaned, and Loots kept driving, barely creeping down the road.

"I shouldn't tell you this," Reid said. "But I know where there is a small cabin not far from here. We could go there until this storm passes."

"No!" Haskins said. "I need to get some medical help."

"I can help you. I'm a doctor," Reid lied.

"Doctors aren't trappers," Haskins said.

"Most all trappers make their living doing something else," Reid said. "Believe me. I can help you."

"Maybe we should listen to him," Loots said. "I think it would be better than trying to drive much farther. We're going to end up in the ditch, or worse."

"Where is this cabin?" Haskins asked.

"Not far. I can direct you. It's going to start getting dark before too long. Then it will really be hard to see."

"You're the one who shot me. Why would you help me now?"

"I didn't mean to shoot you, but when he hit me, the gun just went off. I don't think from where you're hit the wound is bad. But it will need attention soon. There is a larger first aid kit at the cabin. I'm sure I can fix you up."

"C'mon, Maddy," Loots said. "I think we should trust him. We can get out of the cabin as soon as the storm passes."

Haskins thought about it. There was still the question of what to do with Reid, but she was hurting, and if nothing else, she needed some pain reliever.

"Okay," Haskins said.

Reid wasn't positive where they were on the road, but somewhere in the next two miles, there was a spur road that went up to the cabin.

He sat up the best he could in the back seat so he could see better and said, "Watch for a red reflector on the left. It's nailed to a tree about four feet up. Hopefully, we can see it in this snow."

The purple Jeep inched down the road. Luckily, there were ruts in the road where the snow had settled. Loots couldn't see the ruts because of the blinding snow, but he could feel them with the oversized tires.

"It should be along this flat part of the road," Reid said. "Somewhere in here."

A few minutes later, Loots said, "There's a reflector."

Reid looked and said, "That's it. The road is just this side of the reflector."

Loots found an opening in the trees and pulled the Jeep onto a snow-covered dirt road that went gradually uphill.

"The cabin is only two hundred yards up there," Reid said. "If the rig can't make it, we can walk."

The Jeep, with all four big tires pulling and pushing, made it.

Reid noticed that Haskins was being very quiet. Maybe her wound was worse than he thought.

"You're going to need to remove this tape from my wrists and legs," Reid said, sticking his bound wrists between the front seats. "I can't help this way."

"Okay," Haskins said to Loots. "Cut him loose."

With no knife to cut the tape, Loots found one end of the tape on Reid's wrists and unwrapped it. He did the same with the leg wrap. Moving the tape off the broken leg about sent Reid through the roof of the Jeep.

"I'm not sure why you wrapped my legs," Reid said to Loots. "I can't walk anywhere with this broken leg."

"She told me to do it," Loots said. "I've found it best not to argue."

"Help me to the cabin," Haskins barked. "My side really hurts. I need to lay down."

"The door isn't locked," Reid said. "Help her inside and then come back and help me. You can get a fire going, and I can look at the wound."

When Loots and Haskins disappeared inside the cabin, Reid searched through the Jeep. If there was a spare key, he could try to drive out of there and leave them stranded. But he found no keys. They had taken his pack with the pistol and his knife inside when they left the Jeep, but maybe, Reid thought, there would be another gun or knife somewhere in the vehicle he could use to help escape when the storm died down. Again, he found nothing.

In a minute, the big man was marching back through the deep snow to help him out of the truck.

"I'm sorry about all this, Mr. Reid," Loots said as he put his arm around Reid's back to walk him to the cabin. "I had no idea any of this was going to happen."

"You pack a pretty good punch," Reid said.

"Yeah, sorry about that. I just saw you with the gun and figured I needed to do something."

"Don't worry," Reid said. "Once this storm is over, we can get your friend to the hospital."

Inside the old, small cabin, it was dark and smelled like dirty socks.

"There's a propane lantern over there," Reid said. "Matches are on that first shelf."

He instructed Loots on how to get the lantern going, and within a minute it was hissing away, providing some much-needed light.

The cabin looked different than the last time he had been there, Reid thought. Stuff was moved around. If he didn't know better, it seemed like someone had been there recently. Yes, two other trappers used the cabin at times, but they would always leave the place replenished with whatever food they had used. And almost always they would leave a note for the next person, saying who had been there and wishing the next guy good luck.

Reid looked for a note and at the cans of soup and chili on the counter and knew someone other than the trappers had been here. And the place stunk. Someone who really needed a shower had spent some time here, and recently. Luckily, a stack of split firewood sat next to a stone fireplace, more wood than had ever been there before. Once the fire was started, Loots helped Reid over to where Haskins lay on an old couch. Her eyes were closed, and she wasn't moving.

"Is she dead?" Loots asked.

"No, I'm not dead, you dolt," Haskins said. "But I feel like I'm going to die."

"Let me get a look at those wounds," Reid said as he knelt awkwardly next to her and said to Loots, "Grab that red bag off the top of the cupboard."

CHAPTER 15

The gale force wind actually roared as it blew the snow through the trees. Luke had heard people describe the sound of a tornado, and he wondered if this was what it sounded like. It was almost deafening.

He gave his snowshoes to Austin so he could lead the way to the spot where he'd found the firewood earlier. Both men had their heads down and fought the wind and snow every step of the way.

"It's just up here by this stand of firs," Austin yelled to be heard over the wind.

Luke didn't say anything. He just nodded and followed when Austin plodded on. He looked ahead and saw a dark form in a sheet of white that was the group of trees. It was impossible to focus on anything with snow hitting his eyes and face.

When they got to the trees, they began breaking dead branches from under the canopy of the green branches at the bottom of the trees. Most had snow on them, but they were dead-dry underneath the wet snow and would burn well.

Austin moved over to a spot that Luke could see had been disturbed earlier. The young man took the snowshoes off, stuck them in the snow, and began kicking at the ground under the newly fallen snow. Within a few kicks, he displaced a dead lodgepole pine.

He picked the eight-foot log up, turned to Luke, and said, "Pecker poles. There's a bunch of them in this area."

At some point, probably several years ago, a big wind had blown through and knocked dozens of the small trees over. Luke had seen the phenomenon many times. It was like a giant had dropped a container of eight-foot Pick Up Sticks onto the ground. He had walked through such a blow-down twice, and both times it had been a nightmare.

Within a short time, they had scrounged up ten of the lodgepoles and a big armful of the dead limbs. Austin gave Luke the snowshoes and said, "You can wear them back. I'll follow you."

As they dragged the dead trees and branches back to the culvert, it felt to Luke like the storm had gotten worse, which he didn't think was possible.

When they arrived at the makeshift door of the culvert, both men were covered in snow. Because it was blowing into them as they walked, snow and ice encased their clothes in a sheet of white that, when they hit it with their hands, broke into pieces and fell to the ground. Luke pulled the logs into the culvert, while Austin started a fire. Earlier, he had built a fire ring with rocks from the creek and, with the help of some fire starter from his pack, had a crackling fire going within a couple minutes.

The culvert ran north and south into the creek, which helped in keeping the west wind from blowing straight through. Still, some wind and snow snuck through the cracks in the barriers Austin had constructed at each end. The draft worked perfectly in moving the smoke from the fire out of the culvert.

Luke watched as the smoke moved to the south and out some of the spaces between the logs.

"That's how I found you guys," he said. "I saw the smoke coming up from a fire and knew it had to be manmade. I hoped it was you."

"Man, are we glad you did," Jase said. "I couldn't have walked out of here, especially with the deep snow."

With a fire now burning, Luke took a moment to assess their situation. While the culvert was not the optimal shelter, it was better than being out in a tent. This wind could easily take a tent down. The giant metal tube was cold and drafty, but the fire helped.

Luke pulled all the gear out of his pack, including his one-man tent, compact pad, cold weather sleeping bag, down coat, spare waterproof stocking hat and gloves, half-dozen pouches of freeze-dried food, three bottles of water, backpacker's stove with fuel, small pot, energy bars, and the special dog bars for Jack. There were times over the years he'd felt the pack held too much gear and too much weight, but now he was glad he had everything.

"How you doing, Jase?" Luke asked. "You warm enough?"

"I'm good. The fire is helping, and Jack is keeping this side warm," he said, pointing at the dog.

"Well, if you get cold, this sleeping bag is rated to fifteen below, and my puffy coat is extra warm."

"I'm getting kind of hungry," Austin said. "We haven't eaten since this morning."

Luke thought about it and looked at his phone. It was just after five o'clock. He'd eaten the Dairy Queen hamburger a little before noon. It had only been five hours, but it seemed like two days.

"Come to think of it, I'm pretty hungry too," Luke said. "And I bet Jack could eat something."

When he heard his name in the same sentence with 'eat,' Jack raised his head.

"See there," Luke said.

"He's always ready to eat," Austin said with a chuckle.

Luke noticed that one of the young men had a small hatchet out sitting next to the fire pit, and he said to Austin, "I'll work on getting these poles cut down to burning size if you'll cut some meat off the elk quarter."

"Sorry I'm not much help," Jase said.

"Stay still," Luke said. "After we eat, we'll get a splint on the ankle which should help with the pain."

Austin and Jase had backpack stoves, along with a small pot and a spork for each. That would be all they would need to cook up some meat and then be able to eat it.

The little hatchet wasn't the best tool for the job, but in twenty minutes Luke had half of the ten poles cut into two-foot sections and stacked near the fire to dry.

Austin hacked steak-sized chunks of the red meat off the hindquarter. "These aren't the prettiest steaks," Austin said as he worked on the meat with his knife.

"It'll all be good," Jase said. "The meat we had this morning was delicious."

When he had eight steak-size pieces of meat in a large Ziploc bag he'd scrounged from his pack, Austin brought the meat over to the fire.

"We cooked the meat over the fire on a stick this morning," Austin said. "Should we do that again?"

"I'm going to cut some of the meat into smaller pieces and cook it on the Jetboil," Luke said as he was screwing the fuel canister onto the small stove.

In a minute he had the stove burning hot and the meat chunks in the pot with some water and salt and pepper.

Austin cooked one steak medium-rare for Jase, a rare one for Jack, and finally he cooked another medium-rare for himself.

"Pretty danged good," Jase said.

"You shot a good one," Luke said. "Spikes are usually really good eaters."

"Jack seemed to like it," Austin said, nodding at the yellow dog who was now wide awake and watching every bite the men were taking.

"You already had yours," Luke said to Jack.

"I cut a second steak for all of us, including Jack," Austin said.

"Should I cook another for him?"

"Sure," Luke said. "He worked hard today."

They cooked up all the meat, and when it was eaten, they all sat back and let the food settle. Occasionally, a big blast of wind would shake the wood and evergreen branch barriers at one end of the culvert or the other. Snow would come along on the breeze and land around them.

"Man, I'm glad we aren't out in this storm," Austin said.

"Me too," Jase said.

"You guys did good finding this culvert," Luke said. "How'd you sleep last night?"

"We just put on every piece of clothing we had in our packs and laid together next to the fire," Austin said. "It wasn't bad, but we didn't get much sleep either."

"We should take turns tending to the fire," Luke said. "Since you guys need some sleep, I'll take the first shift."

He convinced Jase to take the sleeping bag, and because the bag provided plenty of warmth, Jase gave Austin his heavy coat.

"You can have my coat too if you need it," Luke said to Austin.

"Naw, you put it on. I think I'll be good," Austin said. "Besides, if I put one more article of clothing on, I won't be able to move."

Luke put the puffy coat on, moved closer to the fire, threw a couple more pieces of the pine on the coals, and sat back against his backpack.

Within two minutes, both the young men were sound asleep. Jack was asleep too, lying between Austin and Jase. Another blast of cold air and snow blew through the culvert, but neither of the young men stirred.

Luke poked the fire and sat back. He was glad he had found the young men but would be happier when help arrived. He believed that he and Austin could get Jase back to the car if they had to, but with even deeper snow and drifts created by the blizzard, it would be a struggle. The storm wouldn't last forever, he knew, but he hoped it would end soon, and come morning, help would be on the way.

CHAPTER 16

Reid had seen much worse wounds on soldiers in Iraq, but the bullet holes in Haskins' side could become a problem if she didn't get real medical attention soon. He had cleaned the entrance and exit wounds the best he could and rebandaged them, but that didn't do anything for what might be happening inside her abdomen where the bullet had passed through her. There was a good chance that infection would develop, and if the entire bullet path wasn't thoroughly cleaned and antibiotics started, the situation would become serious.

"Are you going to stitch the holes up?" Haskins asked as Reid was cleaning the wounds.

"No, we need to leave them open for the doctors when we get to the hospital," Reid said. "They're cleaned and bandaged."

"I really hurt," Haskins said with a groan.

Reid looked into the red first aid bag and found some pill

bottles. He knew there was some OxyContin in the bag because he had put it there after having a tooth pulled that then got infected. He had only used a couple of the capsules because the pain from the tooth wasn't all that bad, and he figured it might be good to have some serious pain reliever at the cabin just in case.

Only two other men knew about the cabin, two trappers who would spend a night or two if they were working three or four lines and needed to check the traps every day. He had talked to the other two trappers in the days before he'd come up to check his trapline and knew none of them had been to the cabin in the last month.

When he noticed that someone had been in the cabin recently, he worried they may have found the Oxy. But the bottle was still there, and he gave Haskins two of the pain pills.

"This should help with the pain," he told her. Then he took one of the pills himself. All the movement was aggravating his leg, and it hurt like hell.

"Is this a summer cabin or something?" Loots asked as he put a couple more pieces of the split wood on the fire.

"No," Reid said. "It's used by me and a couple of other guys who run our traplines in this area. I'll stay here sometimes so I don't have to drive all the way back to town if I need to check some traps."

"You are all assholes," Haskins mumbled from the couch. "There is no reason on God's green earth why anyone should be trapping animals anymore."

Reid knew it would do no good to argue with the woman, so he said nothing.

"Looks like there are some cans of food over there," Loots said. "Can we fix something? I'm starving."

"Sure," Reid said. "Why not open a couple cans of that beef stew."

Loots grabbed two cans of Dinty Moore off the shelf, popped open the lids, took one of the three pots that hung on a nail on the wall down, and dumped the stew into the pot. He pulled a bottle of water out of a twenty-four pack of Kirkland-brand bottled water sitting in a corner, opened it, and poured a little into the pot with the stew.

"There's a rack over there you can slide into the fireplace and put the pot on it to heat," Reid said. "Gotta keep an eye on it though—turn it and stir it, or it will burn on one side."

Loots put his full attention on heating the stew.

Haskins had Reid's backpack on the couch with her and had wrapped an arm through it. Now that the fire was warming the little cabin, he could see her eyes drooping. The pain reliever was kicking in too, he thought. If he was going to get out of this thing with nothing more than a broken leg, he needed to get his pistol back. Maybe when she fell asleep, she would let her guard down.

"It's ready," Loots declared after stirring the stew nonstop for a few minutes.

"Bowls are on the shelf, and spoons are in the top drawer," Reid said.

The small cabin didn't really have a kitchen, just one tiny pine wood cabinet with four narrow drawers that sat beneath some wood shelves. There was no sink, but a Rubbermaid tub was placed on top of the cabinet and served as a wash basin for people and dishes.

Loots served up a bowl of stew for Haskins, but when he took it to her, her eyes were closed, so he handed the bowl to Reid.

"I guess she'll eat later," he whispered to Reid when he handed him the bowl.

"Thank you," Reid whispered back. "And would you mind bringing me a bottle of water?"

Loots fetched the water to Reid, then went and served up a bowl of the steaming stew for himself.

After Loots settled in a wooden chair, Reid asked, "So, how long have you had the Jeep?" He figured if he could continue to endear himself to the young man, it might be easier to get out of his situation.

"I bought it two years ago," Loots said. "A friend of mine fixed it up, but then he fell in love with this girl, and she hated it, so he sold it to me."

"Women, huh?" Reid said.

"Huh?" Loots asked.

"Never mind. So whose idea was it to try to catch a trapper in a trap?"

"That was Melissa's idea," Loots said. "She *REALLY* hates trapping!"

"I guess so. And she recruited you to help?"

"No, Maddy asked me," Loots said between bites of potatoes and carrots. "We sat next to each other in biology class. We started talking, and one thing led to another."

"So, you've got nothing against trapping?"

"I hadn't ever thought about it. But it does seem kind of cruel. I mean, if I was a rabbit or something, I wouldn't want to die that way."

Loots was now looking into his bowl and pushing the vegetables around with his spoon. "Isn't there supposed to be some meat in this stew?"

"So, this Melissa recruited Maddy, and Maddy recruited you to help?" Reid asked, swinging the subject back to who all was involved in the scheme.

"Yeah, me and the Prez," Loots said.

"The Prez?"

"Yeah, his name is the same as some president from like fifty years ago, so everyone calls him that."

"You don't know which president?"

"I can't remember," Loots said. "Nobody ever calls him by his real name."

"Kennedy?" Reid asked.

"No, that wasn't it."

"Johnson?"

"No."

"Nixon?"

"Yeah, Nixon, that's it. But everyone just calls him the Prez."

"Just the four of you?" Reid asked. He wanted to have as much information on this bunch as he could gather if, or when, the law got involved. With Haskins asleep and Loots in a talking mood, he would keep trying for more.

"The girls wanted a few more people, but then they decided that the four of us could handle the first mission. That's what they called it—a mission. Kinda like the *Mission: Impossible* movies. I really like those. It felt just like we were in the movies when we were setting those traps."

"So, you set more than one?" Reid asked.

"Yeah, we set another one somewhere up here. The Prez has it marked on his GPS."

"You know the other trapper who you were trying to catch?" Reid asked.

"I never heard the name, but I think Melissa and Maddy knew who it is."

"Did you set the traps at the same time?"

"On the same day, yeah," Loots said. "Me and the Prez set the first one for the other guy, and then the one for you. We came back up yesterday morning and saw your truck and the other guy's truck parked on the road near the trails, so we knew you were up there checking your traps."

"Why did you come back to let me out?" Reid asked.

"Maddy got all worried that you and that other dude might die, what with the big snowstorm. So she wanted to check on you."

"What about the other trapper—did you let him loose?"

"He didn't get caught. Or that's what Maddy said. When we checked where his pickup was parked, it was gone. Yours was still there and covered in snow, so we figured you might be in the trap."

Reid thought about it for a minute. Really, what good did they think this so-called mission was going to do? He wanted to ask Loots that very question, but by talking with him, he figured the big man didn't really have a clue.

"You know," Reid finally said. "If I had died out there stuck in that trap, you guys would all be guilty of murder and would have gone to prison for a very long time."

"Melissa said that wasn't going to happen," Loots said as he scooped a big piece of potato out of the bowl. "She said no one would know it was us who set the traps."

"What's this Melissa's last name?" Reid asked.

"I don't know," Loots said. "I don't think anyone ever said. I know Maddy's last name because I saw it on her quiz sheet in biology. Not that I was copying her answers or anything."

"And?" Reid asked and paused.

"And what?"

"What's her last name?"

"None of your business," Haskins said groggily from the couch. "You need to keep your big mouth shut, Skyler."

"We fixed some beef stew," Loots said, trying to change the subject. "Although it seems to be a little light on the beef. You want some?"

"I'll eat in a minute," Haskins said. "What did you tell him?"

"Just how we set the trap up there and then came to let him go after the snowstorm."

"Okay, well, he doesn't need to know anything else." Then she said to Reid, "You got any more pain relievers? My side is killing me."

The first aid bag was still on the floor next to Reid. He picked it up, found some Aleve, shook three tablets out of the bottle, and handed them to Loots to give to the woman. She didn't need any more Oxy right now.

She took the pills with a big gulp of bottled water and then proceeded to drink the rest of the water. "I might try to eat something," she said.

Loots grabbed another bowl and spoon from the shelf, scooped up a helping of the stew, and delivered it to Haskins.

After watching her eat for a few minutes, Reid said, "So, what's your plan for me? You going to kill me?"

When he said that, Loots turned and looked at Haskins to see what she would say.

"No," she said. "We're against violence. Trapping is violence against innocent animals. We wouldn't kill anything or anyone."

"You say trapping is violence, but you purposefully trapped me. That's kind of talking out of both sides of your mouth, isn't it?"

"Trapping you serves a purpose," Haskins said. "It goes to the greater good."

"I don't see it," Reid said. "All it does is maybe stop me from trapping for six months or a year, until my leg heals."

"When the word gets out that there is an organization that is giving trappers a taste of the pain and horror that they are putting innocent animals through, we'll get national media attention. Most of the people in the big cities around the country have no clue that trapping still exists. They think trappers died off with the passenger pigeon and dodo birds. Once people learn trapping is still going on, they'll contact the lawmakers in Washington, D.C., and eventually we'll get all trapping banned."

Reid was shaking his head. "And you are willing to go to prison for your beliefs?" he asked.

"We won't go to prison," she said. "No one will know it was us who put the traps out."

"I know," Reid said. "So I guess you are going to have to kill me because I sure as hell am going to let the police know what happened."

Loots stood and said, "No one is going to kill anyone." Then he said to Haskins, "You said you didn't want anyone to die. That's why we came up here."

"If we don't get Maddy here to the hospital tomorrow, she could die," Reid said. "So let's think about that."

And they did.

Haskins set her partially eaten bowl of stew down and closed her eyes. Reid lay back and closed his. Loots went to put another log on the fire.

CHAPTER 17

The new day arrived like the previous one had departed, with wind and blowing snow. But, as Luke listened, the intensity of the wind seemed to be waning. It sounded as if the storm was finally running out of energy.

He had nodded off a time or two during the night, but then a big blast of wind, accompanied by a refreshing scattering of snowflakes, would wake him. He kept the fire going, first by burning all the pieces of pine he had cut and then by slowly feeding the longer lodgepoles into the fire. Austin and Jase were dead to the world, and he didn't want to wake them by chopping more firewood.

As he watched the fire, Luke thought about the trapper who had gone missing and the story about the other trapper who had found a leghold bear trap set near his cage traps. In all the years he had been a warden, he had never heard of a trapper going missing.

There had been plenty of lost hunters, or hunters who had died from a stroke or heart attack in the field. But never a trapper.

He had run into, and talked with, a few trappers out in the woods. And he knew two trappers who were on call with the Department of Fish and Wildlife who took care of problem animals. A beaver damming a creek on private property, or a skunk killing chickens would often need to be removed, and WDFW would call the trappers.

Was the lost trapper and the one who found the bear trap a coincidence? He'd have to think about that.

Luke could see the daylight fighting through the cracks of the lean-to doors and decided to go see what they might be up against this morning. He got up and walked to the south end of the culvert, slightly hunched over so as not to bang his head.

Jack, seeing Luke moving, got up, stretched, and followed.

"Hey, boy," Luke whispered. "Let's go see what Mother Nature threw at us last night."

He had to push much harder to get the makeshift door open. The swirling wind had drifted two feet of snow up against it. A few flakes were still coming out of the steel gray sky, but most of the snowflakes in the air had already fallen and were now being picked up and blown around by the wind.

Jack jumped and jumped to get through the snow that, from what Luke could tell, was not much deeper on the flats than it was when they'd walked through it before dark. The hard wind had kept the snow from piling up on the even ground. But he could see there were spots where the snow had collected against the banks of the nearby creek, and the drifts could be four or five feet deep. If he and the young men had to walk through too many drifts like that, they would never make it out to the trucks. They really needed someone to come help them out.

After he and Jack relieved themselves, Jack having to really work to find a spot where he could lift his leg, they headed back into the culvert.

"Hey, Jack!" Jase said as the yellow dog greeted him with a cold, wet nose.

Both young men were awake, and Austin was getting his backpacker's stove set up.

"I'm going to fix Jase some bacon and eggs," Austin said. "You want some, Luke?"

"Sounds good," Luke said. "Could I get a couple of flapjacks with mine?"

"Oooo, wouldn't that be good?" Jase said. "This freeze-dried food is okay for a couple of days, but it would sure be nice to have a big country breakfast."

"We'll do that when we get out of here," Luke said, then to Austin, "I'll wait on mine. I'm going to go text Sara."

Luke grabbed his phone, turned on his Garmin inReach, and headed back out the south entrance of the culvert. When he stepped outside, he noticed that the snow had stopped falling. That boded well for a possible extraction today.

When he was clear of the trees and his inReach was connected to the satellites, his phone buzzed. It was a text from Sara.

Weather reports are favorable. Kittitas Search and Rescue have three members headed up the mountain at 8 a.m. They have your GPS coordinates and should be to you before noon barring any problems.

Luke texted back: *Good to hear. Snow has stopped. Wind is subsiding. We are doing fine. Will look for help this morning. Tell rescue squad to watch for drifts.*

He waited for almost three minutes and then his phone buzzed again:

Glad you are doing well. Will tell KSR. Be safe.

Luke read the text and then headed back to the culvert where Austin was pouring steaming water into a pouch that showed a picture of a big helping of scrambled eggs next to perfectly cooked strips of bacon. The freeze-dried breakfast was palatable, but come on, it wasn't going to be *that* good, Luke thought.

"I'm going to cook up some more elk meat for Jack if that is okay," Austin said.

"Sure," Luke said. "He's going to need his energy today. He can hardly run through that deep snow out there. And if he hits a drift, he'll probably sink out of sight."

He told the young men about the text from Sara and said, "Maybe we should go try to retrieve the rest of the elk meat, Austin. That way we will have it here when help arrives."

"That would also give us meat in case we get stuck here for longer," Austin said.

Luke didn't want to think about that, but he knew Austin was right.

"Let me finish up this delicious breakfast, and then we'll go see if we can find the meat."

"I know right where it is," Austin said. "Plus, I've marked the tree on my GPS, just in case."

"How's your leg this morning?" Luke asked Jase.

"That splint you made seems to be helping. Stopping it from moving around is keeping the pain down, I think."

Luke had taken a couple thin ends of the lodgepoles they had cut for firewood and used them with some tape he had in his backpack to cobble together a splint. When he was done, it looked like a prehistoric walking boot. After putting it on the injured ankle, he'd checked with Jase a couple times to make sure the splint wasn't too tight.

"Good to hear the splint's helping," Luke said to Jase, and then to Austin, "Ok, you ready to go get that meat?"

Luke and Austin took the remaining unnecessary items out of their packs and headed to the door. Jack wanted to go along, but Luke told him to stay.

"You stay with Jase," Luke said to the dog like he would understand. "We'll be back in a while."

Austin put on Luke's snowshoes and grabbed his rifle. Luke picked up his walking poles, and they were out the door.

The walking was much easier for Austin with the snowshoes, but Luke kept up. Occasionally, they'd step into a drift up to their crotch, but mostly the depth of the snow was right at their knees.

It took them a half hour to get to the tree where the meat was hanging.

When they arrived, Austin looked at the meat and said, "Looks like nothing has bothered it. Usually, the scrub jays would have been eating on it by now."

"I think that blizzard kept everything holed up," Luke said. "Or it drove them out of here."

They loaded the second hindquarter in Luke's pack, along with one of the backstraps and some rib and neck meat. Austin took the two front quarters, the second backstrap, and other meat and then strapped the spike bull's head on top of the pack.

When they were all loaded up, this time with Luke in the snowshoes leading the way, they headed back to the culvert. The heavy packs made walking in the deep snow tougher, but by staying in the snowshoe tracks and avoiding the drifts they'd hit on the trip to the meat, they managed to make it back in forty-five minutes.

"I sure hope we don't have to try to walk out of here," Luke said. "That short distance took us almost an hour. Hiking back to the trucks would take all day."

In the next hour the clouds started to break up, and a few rays of sunshine beamed down through the treetops. Luke went out with the satellite communicator one more time and was told by a text from Sara that the Kittitas Search and Rescue people had had trouble getting up the road due to some deep snowdrifts, but they were now on snowmachines and headed their way.

"The Search and Rescue guys are headed our way," Luke said.

"That's good," Jase said. "I feel this ankle swelling, and it's starting to hurt more."

"They should be here soon," Luke said. "Maybe we should fix up some more elk before they get here."

They cooked the venison on sticks over the fire, using up the last of their firewood.

"This sure is good," Austin said, looking at Jase. "Couldn't have shot a better one in my opinion."

Jack watched the guys eat, and each gave him a bite now and

again. He was waiting for his next bite when his ears perked up and he turned to look out the culvert.

"Jack hears something," Austin said. "It must be the guys on snowmobiles."

Luke reached for Jase's rifle just in case. He knew that after the snowstorms every carnivore in the woods would be out looking for something to eat. If a cougar or wolves smelled the elk, they could be coming for a chance at an easy meal.

In thirty seconds, they could hear the drone of the snowmobiles. Luke got up, and he and Jack went out the door and up onto the road where the snow machine operators could see them. Luke saw them before they saw him. There were three men driving snowmachines, and two of the snowmobiles were towing what looked like industrial-sized plastic kids' sleds. He waved his arms, and the lead rider spotted Luke and turned toward him.

A moment later, the three snowmachine riders were stopped on the skid road.

"Glad to see you guys," Luke said. "I'm Luke McCain. The other two are still down in the culvert."

The three men introduced themselves as they jumped off the snowmachines and shook Luke's hand.

"Smells like you got something good cooking down there," a man named Jim Simms said.

"Fresh elk roasted over the fire," Luke said. "It's pretty darned good. There's plenty if you guys are hungry."

"We had Hostess sugar donuts for breakfast," a second man named Mike Matzke said. "Elk steak sounds pretty good for lunch though."

The three men followed Luke and Jack down off the road and to the entrance of the culvert. He introduced Jase and Austin to the men.

"We're pretty happy to see you guys," Jase said, pointing at his foot in the splint. "I thought I might be trapped out here until spring."

"No problem," Simms said as he looked around at the makeshift shelter. "This was a good way to stay out of the snow and wind."

"Wouldn't want to live here," Austin said. "But for a couple of nights it wasn't bad."

Luke carved some steaks off the hindquarter, and the men took the cooking sticks and started roasting the meat over the fire.

"Can we start loading stuff onto the sleds?" Luke asked.

"Here," Simms said, handing Austin his stick. "Cook this for me, and I'll help Luke. There is a way to load those things so they'll ride right."

"Gunna have room for my dog?" Luke asked as he and Simms were heading out of the culvert. "I don't think he's going to be able to run very well in this deep snow."

"We'll figure something out," Simms said. "He might be able to ride on the seat between me and whoever rides shotgun."

Simms grabbed Austin's pack with the elk meat, Luke grabbed his, and they walked up to where one of the black plastic sleds was sitting.

"You're the officer who caught that serial killer up in the North Cascades a couple years back, aren't you?" Simms said. "That was good stuff."

"Yeah, well, you can thank the governor for that," Luke said. "I was just sitting at home, minding my own business, and got the call from the man himself to come help."

They took the meat out of the packs, and Simms placed it purposefully on the sleds.

"Want it heavier in the back," he said. "That way the nose will ride up and not get caught on anything. That's the idea anyway. Still could do a nosedive, so we need to watch 'em."

Back in the culvert after unloading the packs, Luke and Austin refilled them with the items that needed to go back in, including Luke's sleeping pad and bag and extra clothes. They took their packs, along with Jase's, up to the sleds and set them next to the empty sled.

"Wonder if one of us is going to ride in this thing," Austin said.

"Maybe," Luke said. "Or maybe Jack. Although it might be

more comfortable for Jase to ride in it if he can cushion his ankle."

After the men had eaten and they had cleared everything out of the culvert, including the rocks from the firepit, they helped Jase hobble up to the snowmobiles. With his pack as a backrest, they got Jase situated in the second sled with his foot up on Austin's pack and Jack between Jase's legs. With everything strapped down in the first sled, Luke slung Jase's rifle over his head and shoulder and climbed onto the back of Simms' snow machine. Finally, Austin climbed onto the back of Matzke's snowmobile with his rifle. They gave one more look around, fired up the machines, and slowly turned to go back in the direction of the trucks.

Simms, leading the group, took it slowly, and they stopped a few times along the way to check on Jase. His leg hurt, he said, but not much more than it had in the shelter. So, they mushed on.

When they got to Luke and Austin's trucks, they stopped.

"We couldn't get up the road pulling the trailers," Simms said. "So we still have about two miles to go to get to where we're parked. You want to try to drive out?"

"I think it's worth a try," Luke said. "If you can get Jase down to the hospital, we'll catch up to him there."

After again thanking the men, Luke, Austin, and Jack watched the three snowmobiles head down the road with Jase in the sled. They brushed the snow off their trucks, started them, and waited for everything to warm up.

Luke texted Sara to let her know they were back to their rigs and that Jase was headed to the hospital in Ellensburg. Sara texted back, saying she had let Jase's mom know so she could meet him at the hospital. And she had let Jessie Meyers know that Austin was with Luke at their trucks.

"Your mom knows you are back at the trucks with me," Luke said.

"Good, I'll be glad to be home."

"You have chains for your tires?" Luke asked.

"Yes," Austin said. "You think we're going to need them?"

"I think if we inch out of here in low gear, we should be fine,"

Luke said. "But it's good to know you have them if we need them."

"After you," Austin said and jumped in his truck.

As he slowly drove down the road, Luke thought about the past twenty-four hours. He was glad to be headed out of the mountains with the two young men safe. After a bit, his thoughts turned to the lost trapper. He wondered if he had been found, and if not, where he might be.

CHAPTER 18

Steve Reid had had another restless night. His broken leg hurt like the dickens. And his jaw hurt where the big kid had punched him. He took another OxyContin and told himself it would be his last.

The wind roared off and on and pounded away at the little cabin, sometimes sounding like it was going to tear the roof off. Reid imagined this was what it sounded like to be in a tornado in Oklahoma or someplace.

He wanted to get at his backpack where his pistol was stashed, but the woman clutched it to her body like it was her baby. Plus, he couldn't really move with his leg like it was, so even if she had set the pack aside, he probably couldn't get to it.

The kid had helped Reid to the only bed in the cabin, a single bed that sat on a metal frame next to the far wall, which was nice of him. Still, Reid couldn't sleep as he heard everything that was going on outside and in, including the crying calls of Haskins whenever she woke up. She had awakened several times in the night, calling for Loots.

"Skyler, I need some water" or "Skyler, I need more pain pills."

Loots would dutifully get up off the floor, where he had laid out two wool blankets on which to sleep, and get whatever she was asking for.

Once, he came over to Reid and whispered, "How are you doing? You need anything?"

"I'm okay," Reid said.

"That wind sure sounds bad," Loots said. "You think it will quit soon?"

"I don't know," Reid said. "It has to quit sometime. I'm more worried about the snow. If it continues to pile up, we're not getting out of here."

"My Jeep will get us out," Loots said.

"Maybe," Reid said. "But with a blizzard like this, there are going to be some pretty big drifts. About the only thing that'll run in deep, drifting snow is a snowmobile."

"What about Maddy? She needs help."

"We'll try," Reid said. "But we need to see how bad it is come morning."

Loots went back to his blankets on the floor near the fireplace. Reid lay back and thought about their predicament. Even if he did have his pistol, what good was it to have in his possession unless these two decided to kill him with it? He decided to stop thinking about that.

*

The howling wind woke Carter in the middle of the night. The windows in the motel room rattled almost nonstop, and the wind hit the crack under the door just perfectly so it created a high, shrilling whistle. He turned the TV on with the volume up, which helped mask the sounds of the blizzard somewhat, but still it was hard to sleep.

He was getting more and more worried about getting caught. He had been an idiot to rob the liquor store, and shooting that guy, well, that was most likely going to get him a life sentence in Kuna at the Idaho Maximum Security prison, if he was lucky. The electric chair if he wasn't.

If that cashier hadn't pulled his pistol, he would be alive today, and Carter would not be a wanted man. Well, he would be wanted, but not nearly as wanted as a murderer. All for fourteen hundred bucks. If he had stolen that much in California, they would have taken his mug shot, fingerprinted him, and sent him on his way.

But it wasn't California. And it wasn't just fourteen hundred bucks. It was Idaho, where they still had the death penalty for murder.

As he thought about it, maybe he wouldn't try to get to Alaska. Unless he could find a good fake ID, they would get him as soon as he purchased a plane ticket. No, for right now, he needed to lie low. And that little cabin up there away from everything would be the perfect spot to get away.

He walked over to the rattling window and looked out. The snow was blowing sideways, and it was almost blocking out the streetlight only thirty yards away.

Carter shivered at the sight and went back to bed. He wanted to sleep. He needed to sleep. But with everything rolling around in his head and the wind whistling through the door, it was next to impossible.

*

Melissa Short was almost apoplectic. She had called Haskins' cell phone nearly thirty times and had driven to her apartment again. She could not raise her friend.

What made it worse was the local television stations were warning of pending blizzard conditions in the higher elevations of Kittitas and Yakima Counties, and the state patrol said they would most likely be closing all the major passes through the Cascades.

Short called Nixon again. "What are we going to do?" she asked him.

"What can we do?" Nixon asked her back. "We'd be stupid to try to drive up there. We don't have the vehicle for it, and it sounds like it's only going to get worse."

"Should we call the police?" Short asked.

"And tell them what? Our friends have gone to check on some bear traps that we placed illegally in the woods to try to catch some men?"

"No, but we could make something up."

"I guess you could try," Nixon said. "But I'm not sure what anyone is going to do about lost people in a blizzard."

They chatted for a few more minutes, Short said she was going to try to call in a missing person report, and they hung up.

"911, what is your emergency?"

"Yes, I need to report someone being lost, or stranded, in the mountains west of Ellensburg."

The 911 operator asked for Short's name, address, and phone number. Then she asked for the name of the person who was lost.

"It is two people actually." Short gave the operator Haskins' and Loots' names and descriptions.

"They were driving a purple Jeep with giant tires. I don't know the license plate number, but it is the brightest purple you'll ever see."

"Okay," the operator said. "How long have they been missing?"

"Forty-eight hours," Short fibbed. She remembered watching one of those missing people shows on TV where the cops wouldn't do anything until someone had been missing for forty-eight hours. Or that is what she thought she remembered.

"Any idea exactly where they were headed?"

"Not really. The guy, Skyler, loves to drive that Jeep in the snow. He thinks that because it has those oversized tires, it can go anywhere. I'm afraid they've driven off the road or something and can't get out. I'm really worried."

"Okay, Ms. Short. I will let the Kittitas County Sheriff's

Department know. But with this blizzard coming in and the already deep snows from this last storm, it may be a while before they can get up there and look."

"Can you call me if you hear something?"

"I'll ask the sheriff's department to call you if they learn anything."

Short thanked the operator and hung up. At least she had done something, although it didn't sound like it was going to do much good.

She called Nixon back and told him what had transpired with the call to 911. He wanted to say, 'I told you so' but said instead, "Well, at least they'll be looking for them at some point. I'm guessing we'll be hearing from Maddy soon."

"I don't know," Short said. "But I'm starting to get a really bad feeling."

CHAPTER 19

Reid pushed himself up, hopped on one foot over to the one small window in the cabin, and saw daylight streaming through a crack in the curtains. It was still snowing lightly, and the wind was blowing, but not as hard as it had been during the night.

"Is it still snowing?" Loots asked in a sleepy voice.

"Yes, but it has lightened up considerably," Reid said.

He looked at Haskins and wondered how she was feeling. He didn't have to wonder long.

"We need to get to the hospital," she said without opening her eyes. "My insides are on fire, and the bullet wound hurts like hell."

"Let me check the bandages," Reid said, hopping over to where she lay on the couch. Every time he hopped, a shock of pain went up his leg, then up his back, and finally it would register in his brain like the whack from a ball-peen hammer.

Reid helped her roll onto one side and looked at the bandage on her back. It was totally drenched with blood. Then he rolled her back and checked out the bandage in front. It was not as bad. He was glad to see the blood was still red and there was no sign of infection . . . yet.

"I need to change the bandages. Come help me, Skyler."

Loots helped Haskins sit and held her sweater up so that Reid could remove the bandages.

After cleaning the wounds, Reid packed some gauze in them and then covered each with a large pad and taped them down.

"Can I have more pain pills?" she asked Reid.

"Yes," Reid said and then asked Loots to grab two more Oxys out of the first aid bag.

"We really need to get her to the hospital," Loots said. "Do you think we should try to go now?"

"We could try," Reid said. "But I think it's risky."

Loots put on his boots, coat, and hat and headed for the door.

"I'm going to go warm up the Jeep and get it ready to roll."

"Okay," Reid said.

Haskins just moaned.

When he returned, Loots helped Haskins get bundled up in her coat and hat. Instead of making her walk, he picked her up, walked to the door, opened it, and disappeared with her in his arms out into the blowing snow.

Reid saw that Haskins had left his backpack on the couch. He hopped over to it, grabbed his pistol, and tucked it into his pants at the small of his back. Then he put on his coat, stocking cap, and gloves and waited for Loots to return.

Two minutes later, Loots was back.

"She told me to grab the backpack on the couch," Loots said.

"Too late," Reid said. "I have the gun, but I have no intention of using it."

Loots looked at Reid's face to see if he was telling the truth.

"I'm serious, Skyler. I won't use it. I just wanted it in my possession so you or Maddy won't use it on me."

Loots thought about bull rushing Reid, as he had done before, but that would only slow them down. He'd try for the gun later. Maybe.

"Okay. Let's go," Loots said as he walked to Reid to help him to the Jeep. "I think the wind is dying, and the snow is letting up, for sure."

Loots had arranged Haskins on the back seat so she could lie down. Reid sat in the passenger seat.

"I'd take it very slowly," Reid said as Loots started to back the Jeep in an arch. "Deep snow hides all kinds of trouble up here."

The words were barely out of Reid's mouth when the back of the Jeep dropped into a hole.

Loots put the rig in low gear and tried to drive out of it, but the back wheels were not in contact with anything solid and the front wheels were just spinning in the deep, wet snow.

"This is not good," Loots said as he tried to back the Jeep up and then pull forward. The vehicle didn't move an inch.

Loots got out of the Jeep and looked at the rear of the rig. Reid saw the big man scratch his head and then walk to the front and look at it.

Loots came back to the driver's door and said, "Maybe we can dig it out, but I don't know. I think someone is going to have to give us a pull."

From the back of the Jeep, Haskins said, "And who will that be, Skyler? Nobody is driving up here right now, and can anyone even see this place from the road?"

"No, they can't," Reid said. He thought about his truck, just up the road, but didn't say anything. If they didn't remember, it would be better for him.

Nobody said anything for a minute, and then Reid said, "Our only hope of getting help sometime soon is to have Skyler walk out and call for help. There's a spot only a mile or two down the road where most cell phones can get some service. Is your phone charged?"

"Yeah, it shows some battery power," Loots said. "But I don't know. I hate to leave you guys here."

"Get us back into the cabin," Reid said. "We'll be okay. But you are going to have to hurry. The weather is letting up, so someone should be able to give us help even if they have to come on snowmobiles."

Ten minutes later, Haskins was on the bed, and Reid was sitting with his leg up on the couch. Loots had stoked the fire with three split logs, brought two bottles of water, and gave them each a wax paper sleeve of Ritz crackers from a box he found on the shelf.

"I'm not worrying about starving to death," Haskins said after he brought the crackers over to her. "I'm worrying about dying from some horrible infection."

Loots said nothing and just turned and headed to the door.

"Thanks, Skyler," Reid said. "You'll do fine."

When he was gone, Haskins said, "My life is in that big dummy's hands. You really think this will work?"

"What other choice do we have?" Reid said. "Surely, he is smart enough to be able to walk down the road and make a call."

"How is he going to know where to tell the ambulance, or whatever might be coming, where we are?"

Reid hadn't thought about that.

"I don't know. Hopefully, he can figure it out."

"Hopefully," Haskins said. But she didn't sound very hopeful.

*

Loots walked down the road slowly, because each step was a chore. The snow was at least two feet deep everywhere, and sometimes it was three feet or more if it had drifted. Still, he knew he had to get to cell service to be able to help Maddy.

He wanted to help Reid too. After spending time with the man, Loots had decided he wasn't all that bad, and now he was sorry he had helped set the trap that hurt Reid's leg. And he was sorry he'd hit him.

Although, as he thought about it more, he kind of had to hit Reid, because he *had* pulled a gun on them. Now, Reid had the gun again. He wouldn't shoot Haskins again, would he? Loots thought about that and other stuff, like how his Jeep had gotten stuck, and how he was going to get it unstuck.

As he walked, the wind died down to nothing, and soon the gray snow clouds were starting to break up. The sun popped out occasionally, making the snow sparkle. That made him feel better.

Loots would check his phone every fifteen minutes or so as he walked, and finally after checking it eight times—he knew it was eight times because he was keeping track so he could tell Maddy when he saw her again—he saw the small bars in the upper corner of the screen on the phone were filled in. He stopped and dialed 911.

After the 911 operator got his name and phone number, she asked what his emergency was.

"My friends and I are stuck up in the mountains. Well, one is a friend and the other man, well, he is stuck with us."

"Where in the mountains?"

"Um, well, we are past Cle Elum," Loots said.

"You are going to have to do better than that, Mr. Loots."

"We are on the left side of the freeway, up a Forest Service road about nine or ten miles."

"Any idea what the Forest Service road number is?"

"I didn't know they had numbers," Loots said.

"Can you ask one of your friends?"

"No, I just walked for two hours to get phone service. They are up by my stuck Jeep, and both are hurt. One has a bad leg, probably broken, and the other was shot by a pistol in the side."

"So, you need medical help?"

"Yes, ma'am. That is why I'm calling."

After finding out from Loots that he had seen no vehicle tracks on the road he was on and that the snow was very deep, she said, "We will send snowmobiles to help extract the hurt people as soon as we can figure out where you are."

"I'm sorry, I just don't know," Loots said. "What if I keep walking until I either run into another vehicle or see a sign that says what road I am on, then I can call you again?"

"That will work, I guess," the operator said. "And I will get a medical team headed up that way now. Keep your phone on, and I'll see if we can track it to figure out where you are."

"Okay," Loots said. He said goodbye, clicked off, and kept walking.

When he looked at his phone again, he had no service, and his battery indicator showed he was just about out of power. Now he faced a real dilemma. Should he turn his phone off to save what little battery he had left? Or should he leave it on so the 911 operator could track him and risk losing all power? He tried to figure that one out, but it made his head hurt.

Finally, he decided to leave the phone on and hope the authorities located him and his phone before it went totally dead. He didn't think about what could happen if he just kept walking and no one showed up before it got dark.

Unfortunately, Loots' phone went stone cold dead not ten minutes later.

CHAPTER 20

I t took some steady driving, and about two hours longer than if the roads had been dry, but Luke, followed by Austin, made it down to where traffic had beaten the snow down in the roads. Then they hit pavement that had been plowed at some point. A few minutes later, they were on the freeway headed to Ellensburg.

As he drove, Luke used the hands-free Bluetooth in his truck to call Sara.

"I'm glad to hear your voice," she said after answering the phone. "That satellite texting is all good and fine, but hearing your voice, now I know you are really safe."

"Good to talk to you too," Luke said. "We're going to run by the hospital to check on Jase, and then I'll be on my way home."

"About that," Sara said. "Captain Davis wants you to call when you can. It seems that trapper is still up there not far from where you were. Something weird is happening. Give Bob a call and then call me later."

"That's strange," Luke said. "I've thought about that guy a time or two during the last twenty-four hours. I hope he's okay."

"Call Bob," Sara said. "I love you."

"Love you too," Luke said but quickly realized he was talking to no one. His beautiful wife had hung up on him.

"At least she told me she loved me before she hung up," Luke said to Jack, who was in his normal spot, sleeping away in the seventy-degree warmth of the back seat. Luke looked at him via the rearview mirror and again said, "Some friend you are."

Luke next dialed up Davis.

"Hi, Cap. What's up?"

"Hey, Luke. Sounds like you got those boys out of the mountains."

"I found them, but the Kittitas Search and Rescue guys got us out to our trucks. And they are taking Austin's buddy to the hospital. I think he dislocated his ankle. Probably going to need surgery."

"Ouch," Davis said. "Well, I'm glad you made it through that blizzard and are out of the mountains."

"Sara said there might be something up with that trapper that is lost up here someplace?"

"Yeah, his wife is worried sick. She says he is a very capable mountain man. He's been trapping up there for twenty years or more. She hasn't heard word one from him."

"Okay, so is anyone doing anything?"

"That blizzard, as you know, made it pretty much impossible until this morning, but the real problem is no one knows specifically where he runs his traplines."

"And?" Luke asked after a long pause from Davis.

"And," Davis said, "there is the whole situation with this other trapper, Sam Anderson, who is adamantly claiming that someone set a bear trap on one of his lines right before the first snowstorm. He believes it was purposefully set to catch him. It doesn't take too much imagination to think it may not be a coincidence, and the first trapper, Steve Reid is his name, might actually be trapped up there somewhere."

"Too much to be a coincidence," Luke said. "And I don't have much of an imagination at all."

"Anderson lives in Thorp. Could you go by and talk to him? A Kittitas sheriff's deputy talked to him but basically told him there was no crime there, other than the fact that someone set an illegal leghold trap, and that falls under our jurisdiction."

"I'm just about at the Thorp exit now," Luke said. "I got his number earlier. I'll give him a call and stop to chat with him before I go to the hospital."

"Thanks, Luke," Davis said. "Let me know what you are going to do."

"Will do," Luke said and clicked off.

Luke looked up the number he had received for Sam Anderson and punched the numbers into his phone.

"Hello?" a man's voice said.

"Mr. Anderson?"

"Yes."

"This is Luke McCain. I'm an officer with the Department of Fish and Wildlife. I was wondering if you would have a couple minutes to talk to me if I stopped by your place. I'm actually in Thorp now, just passing that big fruit stand next to the interstate."

Anderson was happy to hear from Luke and told him how to get to his place. "It's got a big bear trap hanging off the center of the entry arch. You can't miss it."

Luke told him he would be there in five minutes, and he was. When he pulled into the driveway, Anderson came out on the porch. The man was tall and fit, probably in his early sixties, Luke thought. A shock of silver hair fell across his forehead from under the bill of a hat with a Chevy bowtie logo on it. The man's eyes looked like they might have been blue in his early years, but now they were steel gray. Like Paul Newman's, Luke thought. Permanent smile lines were etched into his face near his eyes and mouth. He looked like a man who had lived a fruitful and very satisfying life.

Luke jumped out of the truck, told Jack he would only be a few minutes, like the dog could tell time, and hustled over to the steps of the porch.

"Is that that famous yellow dog you got in the truck?" Anderson asked with the smile Luke knew was there.

"Oh, you know about him?"

"Most folks do, I suspect, what with the killers and poachers he's helped run down."

"I don't know about that, but we try not to talk too much about it around him. He gets a big head and demands to be fed all the time."

Anderson chuckled. "Well, he can come on in and warm up next to the fire if you're okay with that. My wife would love to meet him too."

Luke went back and coaxed Jack out of the truck. The dog stretched, wandered over, peed on the light post next to the plowed driveway, and headed for the front door.

"How do you like him now?" Luke asked after the men watched Jack water down the light post.

"Oh, he's just being a dog," Anderson said.

Anderson introduced Luke to his wife Kathy, who said she was happy to meet Luke but was really happy to meet Jack. She already had a cookie of some kind in her hand and gave it to Jack. He happily ate it and looked around for more.

Mrs. Anderson looked like she could be her husband's sister. Not nearly as tall, but every bit as lean, with the same silver hair and smile lines. Her eyes were still a youthful blue, and they sparkled when she looked at Luke. He had heard about couples who started to look alike after years of living together but thought it was more a resemblance in movements and speech patterns that made them seem similar. Not these two, Luke thought. They actually did look alike.

"You're being rude," Luke said to Jack after he ate the cookie. "Go lay down by the fire."

And he did.

"My, he's well-trained," Kathy Anderson said, genuinely impressed.

"Thanks for coming by," Sam Anderson said. "I talked to the local deputy, but if he doesn't see someone actually loading a bunch of televisions still in the Walmart boxes into a U-Haul trailer, he's not going to break a sweat doing anything about anything."

"Tell me what happened," Luke said.

Anderson went through the whole story. He was checking one of his traplines and spotted the chain on the tree. Hadn't been there two days before, he said. Followed the chain to the trap, which was sort of camouflaged next to the trail where he'd placed one of his traps. Sprung the trap and put it in the tree that was wrapped with the chain.

"It's still there if you want to see it," Anderson said. "Although after that blizzard last night, it might be hard to get to."

"I spent the night out in that blizzard," Luke said.

Both the Andersons' faces immediately changed to a look of disbelief. So Luke told them the story.

"Gee, you guys were lucky to find one of those culverts," Sam Anderson said. "I've seen where they've put some of those in around the watersheds near where the Forest Service is allowing logging. Something about helping the fish."

"I bet those boys were glad to see you," Kathy Anderson said.

"Yes, they were. It really wasn't terrible. We had a good fire, ate some roasted elk. They had good, warm, waterproof clothing, as did I. We did fine."

Both the Andersons were shaking their heads.

"So, have you heard about another trapper, Steve Reid, being lost up there in the mountains?" Luke asked.

"We sure have. I don't know Steve well, but I see him at the tanner's place now and again. Us trappers kind of have a brotherhood, and while we are competitors, we're friendly about it."

"My captain raised the question about the chances there might have been two bear traps set up there, and maybe Mr. Reid didn't see the chain around the tree before it was too late like you did?"

"I've been thinking the same thing," Sam Anderson said. "And it makes me madder than a bunch of hornets."

"I know you all are pretty secretive about where you run your traplines, but do you have any idea where Mr. Reid is running his?"

"I have a general idea," Anderson said. "I've seen his truck a time or two heading farther south from where I run mine. I could show you where on a map."

Anderson got up, walked out of the kitchen and down the hall.

"I'm sorry," Mrs. Anderson said. "I've forgotten all my manners. Can I get you something hot to drink? Coffee, tea, hot chocolate?"

"How about a cup of hot chocolate?" Luke said. "I've been craving something like that since we were sitting in the middle of that big culvert."

"Coming right up," she said.

Sam Anderson came back with a long roll of paper and spooled out a large Forest Service map onto the kitchen table. Luke walked over and looked as he pointed out where he ran his traps.

"Been trapping those same areas for years," Anderson said. "Helps pay some bills and keeps me fit. I love being in those mountains."

Then he pointed to a couple different small drainages to the south on the map and said, "If I had to guess, I would say this is where Steve is running his lines."

Luke followed the lines that indicated the Forest Service roads and noted their numbers.

"I've checked hunters up in that area several times over the years," Luke said, "so I know pretty well where those are."

"You'd probably need snow machines to get up there today," Anderson said. "I don't think I could get to my traps right now."

"I have the names of the Search and Rescue guys who came in and picked us up this morning. I'll give them a call. If they can't do it, I bet they would know someone who could."

"Here's your cocoa," Kathy Anderson said as she delivered a steaming mug to Luke, along with a plate of some freshly baked chocolate chip cookies.

Luke took a sip and said, "Mrs. Anderson, this is the best hot chocolate I've ever tasted." Then he took a bite of a cookie, chewed, and made a "Mmmmm" yummy sound. "And the cookies, oh my gosh. When I tell my wife I met the most beautiful woman and she made the best cocoa and chocolate chip cookies I have ever tasted, she's going to hate you. And she's never even met you."

Kathy Anderson laughed, and Luke saw her blue eyes sparkle again.

"You're just saying that, but I appreciate it."

Actually, the cookies truly were right up there with the best he'd ever had. Jack saw Luke eating another cookie and came over to see if he could get in on the action. Kathy Anderson obliged. Jack gobbled it up in two gulps.

"You didn't even taste that!" Sam Anderson said.

Luke smiled. He said the same thing to Jack just about daily.

They chatted for a few more minutes while Luke finished his hot chocolate, with two more cookies, and then he said, "Thanks so much for everything. I'll let you know what I find out about Mr. Reid. I'm heading to the hospital in Ellensburg, but if I can get some snowmobile guys from Search and Rescue, I'll be heading back up the hill."

"What are you going to do with Jack?" Kathy Anderson asked.

"I'm going to send him home with the other young man who came out of the mountains with me this morning. He's my next-door neighbor, so he can deliver Jack to our house."

Mrs. Anderson looked disappointed.

"Well, if that doesn't work out, he can stay with us while you're up there. It's nice to have a dog in the house again."

Luke loaded Jack into the back seat of the truck, waved to the Andersons who were standing on the porch, and drove out of the driveway.

CHAPTER 21

Luke hadn't gotten contact information from the men who had come up that morning on snowmobiles, but he did remember their names. The guy who seemed to be in charge of the group was Jim Simms. Luke scrolled through his contact list on his phone and found the number for the Kittitas County Sheriff's Office and pushed the call button.

The deputy who answered the phone was Alivia Hernandez. Luke had worked with her a time or two over the years, and he liked her.

"Hey, Hernandez, this is Luke McCain."

"Hey, Luke," Hernandez said. "Long time no talk. Whatcha up to today? Running down another serial killer?"

Luke was used to the jab. There were members of the different police departments in the region who liked to give him a hard time about some of the unwanted publicity he had received when he and Jack had tracked down a serial killer and brought him in while being televised live on all the national news networks a couple years back. A few of the officers, Luke knew, were jealous. Most just liked to razz him. Hernandez was a razzer.

"Yeah, you want to go help?" Luke asked.

"I would but I have to go see a guy about a horse," Hernandez said.

"Take your phone into the bathroom then," Luke said. "You can still talk in there, can't you?"

She laughed. "No, I really need to go see a man about a horse. He has a stallion that somehow keeps jumping out of a corral and is pestering the neighbor's mare."

"Sounds like fun. What I'm calling about is I need to contact your Search and Rescue folks. I don't know if Jim Simms is the guy I need to talk to, but I'm going to need a lift up into the mountains on a snow machine."

"Jim would be the guy," Hernandez said. "Didn't he just get back from rescuing you?"

"I wouldn't call it a rescue," Luke said in a high-pitched voice, drawing out the 'I'. "But yes, he came and hauled me and a couple young guys, one who was injured, out of the Taneum this morning."

"Sounds like a rescue to me," Hernandez razzed.

"I'm trying to find that trapper who has been missing since Saturday, and I think I know where he might be, but I'll never make it up there in my truck."

"We were just talking about that guy. Steven Reid. His wife keeps calling. Now that the blizzard is over, I think Search and Rescue is planning a search, but she hasn't given them much to go on about where he might be."

They chatted for another minute, Hernandez gave Luke the number for Simms, and she wished him good luck.

"I hope Mr. Reid is okay," Hernandez said.

"Me too," Luke said. "Good luck with your stud."

"It's a stallion," Hernandez said and rang off.

Luke quickly dialed up Simms and waited for an answer.

"This is Simms," the man said in a way a federal agent might answer a phone.

"Hey, Jim. Luke McCain calling."

"Hey, Luke. We got young Mr. Schlagel to the emergency room. His mom was there waiting. Very glad to see him."

"Yeah, thanks for doing that. I don't even want to think about having to walk out in that snow, so I really appreciate you guys coming in and picking us up."

"No problem. We enjoy doing it."

"The reason for my call is I'm going to need more help from your group," Luke said. "You've heard about that missing trapper, I assume?"

"Yes, we have. We were all set to try to run up there and look for him, then the blizzard hit. There are about a hundred square miles up there in the Taneum, and we have no idea where to start."

"That's why I'm calling," Luke said. "I think I have a pretty good idea where he might be. With the help of another trapper, we think we've located his traplines off Forest Service Road 4110. Any chance you could get a couple guys to run up there with me to take a look?"

"I think we can make that happen," Simms said. "But we're working on another interesting situation. A guy called 911 and said he and two other people, one with a gunshot wound, another with a broken leg, are stuck up in that area too. The problem is the guy had walked out to get phone service and had no idea where he was. We've tried to call him back, but the phone must be dead."

"That is interesting," Luke said. "Did you get any names?"

"Just the guy who called. His name is Skyler Loots, and the even more interesting thing is the sheriff's department got a call from a woman in Ellensburg yesterday who wanted to file a missing person's report. One of the names she mentioned as missing was Loots."

"Okay?" Luke said.

"And he was supposed to be with another person, a woman named Maddy Haskins. But the woman caller said nothing about a third person with them."

"So," Luke said after thinking about it for a minute, "the guy, this Loots, who called in from up there, might be lost himself?"

"That's a possibility," Simms said.

"How do you want to handle this?" Luke asked.

"Well, if you feel like you have an idea where to look for the trapper, I say that's a good place to start. I'll call Matzke, and we'll get gassed up and turn around and head up there. Where do you want to meet?"

Luke felt confident he could get up to the spot where the men had parked their rigs with the snowmobile trailers earlier and said he would meet them there.

"I have to run to the hospital and drop my dog off, but I can probably be back up there in a couple of hours."

"That only leaves about an hour of daylight," Simms said. "But if we can find the trapper and keep him from having to spend another night out there, it would be worth the effort."

Luke said he would see them up there and clicked off.

*

When Luke arrived at the hospital, he found Austin and Jase Schlagel's mom sitting in the emergency room waiting area.

"They're supposed to be bringing Jase out now," Mrs. Schlagel said. "They put his ankle in a cast, and we're supposed to see an orthopedic surgeon in Yakima tomorrow."

"Can you take Jack home with you?" Luke asked Austin. "I'm headed back up in the mountains to try to help find a trapper that's been lost for a few days."

"You won't need him?" Austin said.

"I'd like to have him," Luke said. "But we're going to be on snowmobiles, and that snow is just too deep for him."

"I'm taking off as soon as Jase comes out," Austin said, "so let's go load him in the truck."

They were just about to walk out of the waiting area when Jase was rolled out in a wheelchair by a nurse.

"Looks like they got you in a real cast," Luke said.

"Yeah, the one you built last night got lots of looks from the doctors and nurses. They asked if Fred Flintstone made it."

Everyone laughed, and then Jase said, "But the doctor who removed it was actually pretty impressed. He said to tell whoever did it that they did a good job. So, good job, Luke."

"Well, I'm glad you got a real cast and you can sleep in a warm bed tonight."

They talked for another couple of minutes. Jase's mom thanked Luke about eleven times. Austin and Jase said it was a fun adventure, but they'd maybe wait a year or two before they did it again. Finally, Luke and Austin walked out to Luke's truck, coaxed Jack out of the back seat, and loaded him into the back seat of Austin's truck.

"Sara should be home when you get there," Luke said. "But if not, just take him to your house and she'll grab him when she comes home."

"Will do," Austin said. "And, I know Jase's mom said it, but thanks again for coming to find us."

*

When Luke was back on the road, heading west on I-90 toward Cle Elum, he called Sara.

"As you suspected, I'm not coming home quite yet," Luke said. "I talked to the other trapper, the one who found the bear trap set near his trapline, and he showed me where he believes the missing trapper runs his traps. So I'm going to meet the Search and Rescue guys, and we're going to run up there on snowmobiles and take a look around."

"What about Jack?" Sara asked.

"He's with Austin. They should be home in a half hour or so."

"Okay. Good luck. Stay in touch. Is your satellite texter still charged?"

"Yep, it's good for several more hours."

"Good. Be careful. Love you."

"Love you too," Luke said. This time she didn't hang up until after he'd said it.

When he was done talking with Sara, Luke called Davis again and told him about meeting with Sam Anderson and what the plan was with Search and Rescue.

"Hope you find him," Davis said. "Good luck and let me know what happens."

"Will do, Cap," Luke said and pushed the hang up button on the truck's Bluetooth.

Phone calls taken care of, Luke started thinking about everything. Strange things were afoot. There had to be some connection with the trap that Anderson had found and Steve Reid going missing. But did the man named Loots fit into the puzzle somewhere? And what did Simms say, one of the people that Loots was with had a gunshot wound? And the other person had a broken leg? What the hell happened up there?

He decided to make one more call back to Hernandez. He asked the person who answered the phone to connect him with the deputy, and when she came on the line, Luke said, "How's that stallion?"

"What now, McCain? You think I have nothing better to do than talk to you on the phone?"

"I just missed our witty repartee," Luke said.

"Ah bullsh—" Hernandez cut herself short. "Sorry, the sergeant is in the room, and he does NOT like cursing in the office."

"Hey, Jim Simms said you guys got a call from a woman who reported two people missing up southwest of Cle Elum and that one of the people who was missing was the one who called in a while ago but didn't know where he was."

"Yes, we're trying to reach the guy, Lutz or Loots, but he's not answering his phone."

"Can you get me the phone number for the woman who called in the missing person's report? I'd like to talk to her."

"Give me a second," Hernandez said.

Luke could hear fingers clicking on a computer keyboard, then she came back and said, "Her name is Melissa Short." She gave Luke Short's phone number and address.

"I can't go see her because I'm headed back up into the mountains," Luke said, "but I am going to call her. Something weird is going on. Maybe she can shine some light on it."

"Good luck," Hernandez said. "Now I'm going to see a man about a dog."

"I'm not even going to ask," Luke said and hung up.

CHAPTER 22

Carter waited until the very last minute to check out of his room. Actually, he didn't really check out, he just left the key on the desk by the TV and went to his truck.

He'd eaten a couple of stale Pop-Tarts for breakfast and was hungry, so he drove up the main road, found a Wendy's, and pulled through the drive up. Afterwards, he pulled into a parking spot, ate his double cheeseburger and his Frosty, and worried that people in every car that went by were looking right at him.

There was plenty of snow on the ground in town, and he was worried there might be too much for him to make it up the mountain roads to the cabin. He figured he would kill some time around town, then try to get up the road later in the afternoon, possibly giving others time to drive up that way, breaking a trail. Otherwise, he might have to come back to the motel again tonight and wait for tomorrow.

After his early lunch, Carter went back to the Safeway store to stock up on supplies for the cabin. He bought a six-pack of Pepsi, some bologna and bread, some chips, and a bag of Oreos and sat in his truck and watched the people come and go.

*

After walking another mile, or two, or three—Loots didn't know how far—he was getting very tired and frustrated from walking in the almost knee-deep snow. His phone was dead, and he had no idea where he was. He had looked for some kind of sign or marker that told him what road he was on, but he finally realized it would do him no good if he couldn't talk to someone to tell them where he was.

It finally dawned on him that as soon as he'd seen that his phone was dead, he should have turned around and walked back to the cabin. Haskins would be really upset that he hadn't been successful in getting help on the way, so maybe it was good he wasn't at the cabin.

What he was hoping for now was that a truck or someone out riding their snowmobile might come along. He had told the 911 operator they were lost and hurt. Hopefully, the officials would send someone to look for them, even if they didn't know where he was, or where Maddy and Mr. Reid were.

Not knowing what else to do, Loots found a stump, brushed eighteen inches of snow off it, and sat down.

*

Reid felt helpless. He couldn't walk. His leg hurt like crazy. When she wasn't sleeping, the girl was constantly moaning and asking for help. He felt bad about shooting her, but then again, they did set that trap on him. Now that he had spent some time with them, he didn't believe they were going to kill him, but at the time he'd pulled his pistol and shot her, he hadn't known that.

All he could do now was keep the fire going so they didn't freeze to death and try to help her when she cried for more pain pills or water.

He'd stopped giving her the OxyContin every time she wanted another pill because there were only five pills left. He would give her three or four ibuprofen or Aleve, and that would help some. If she really screamed in pain, then he would give her an Oxy.

Sending Loots out for help was a risk, but it was really the only option they had as far as he could tell. He seemed like a nice kid, but Loots wasn't going to be setting any records on the Mensa test.

Now that they were in the cabin, Reid wasn't worried about his life. His situation was much improved from just a day ago. Yes, he needed to have his leg looked at. But right now, his main concern was for Haskins. He didn't believe the bullet wound was terribly serious, but then again, he had seen a soldier in Iraq die from a bullet wound to his leg. She really needed to get to a hospital.

He thought about trying to walk back to his truck, but his leg just wouldn't make it possible. All he could do was wait and hope Loots was successful in getting some help on the way. And the sooner they got there, the better.

*

Melissa Short answered on the first ring.

"Hello?" she said in a hopeful voice.

"Ms. Short, my name is Luke McCain. I'm a police officer with the Department of Fish and Wildlife."

"Did you find them?" Short interrupted. "Did you find Maddy and Skyler?"

"No, ma'am. Not yet. But that is why I'm calling," Luke said. "Can you give me any more information about what they were doing in the mountains?"

"I think they just went for a ride in Skyler's Jeep," she lied. "It has those big, oversized tires, and he likes to drive places just to see if he can go where other trucks can't."

"Okay. Did the sheriff's office tell you that Mr. Loots called in looking for help?"

"No, they didn't. Are they okay?"

"Well, I'm not sure. He didn't seem to know where he was, and he was on foot. He told the 911 operator that they got stuck and he was walking down the road trying to get cell service. But he had no idea what road they were on, so he couldn't tell the operator where to send help."

"Ah geez," Short said. "Why would she send that idiot to get help?"

"Well," Luke said, "he told the operator that he was with two people, one who had a gunshot wound and another who had a broken leg."

Luke heard Short gasp, and then there was silence.

"You mentioned Maddy. Any idea who the other person is with them?" Luke asked.

More silence.

"Ms. Short?"

"Sorry," Short said. "No, no idea, but oh my God, do you think Maddy has been shot?"

"I don't know, but we would really like to find them, so anything you can tell us would be very helpful."

More silence.

"Do you know if Maddy or Skyler own a firearm? A rifle or a pistol?"

"Not that I know of. Maddy is against any kind of violence. And Skyler, well, maybe, but he never said anything to me about owning a gun."

"Do you know, or have you ever heard, the name Steve Reid?"

Another long pause and then, "No, I don't think so."

After years of checking hunters and anglers, some of whom had caught a few fish over the limit or had broken the law in some other way, Luke had developed a pretty good ear for a lie when he heard it. And he was hearing one now. So he pushed it.

"We are of the opinion that someone has been setting bear traps in the woods specifically targeting trappers. Mr. Reid is a trapper, and we think he may have stepped in one of these traps."

"I know nothing about that," Short said.

Way too defensive and way too fast, Luke thought.

"Well, we are going to get to the bottom of this, Ms. Short. The people who have done this are in very big trouble. If Mr. Reid did get caught in a trap that was purposefully set and died out there in the woods during the blizzard, murder charges will be filed against everyone involved. So if you know anything at all, please let me know."

She again told Luke she didn't know a thing about any trapping or trappers and was just worried about her friends.

"I'm calling from my cell phone, so you have my number," Luke said. "Or you can call the sheriff's office too if you can think of anything else. I hope your friends are okay. And I hope they aren't involved in anything illegal."

After hanging up, Luke thought maybe he shouldn't have pushed it so hard with Short. But she *was* lying about something. He was sure of that.

*

"Oh my God, Rick," Short said as soon as Nixon answered his phone. "I just talked to some cop, and they are on to us. And I think Maddy has been shot."

"What?" Nixon said. "Slow down and tell me what he said."

"This cop just called me and said he heard from Skyler who was walking down a road, and he said that he was lost with two people, and one of them had been shot, and the other one had a broken leg."

"That makes no sense," Nixon said. "Were the other two with Loots walking down the road?"

"I don't know," Short said. "All I heard was someone was shot, and it must be Maddy."

"Who the hell is the third person?"

"Probably that trapper guy," Short said. "He could be the person with the broken leg if he stepped in the trap."

"So, Skyler called for help?"

"Yeah, but he said they were stuck, and he was walking down a road but had no idea where he was."

"Well, we know where," Nixon said. "Or at least we have a good idea. Shouldn't we tell the cops where to find them?"

"I don't know. The cop said that they know about the traps, and everyone involved with setting them is in serious trouble, and if the trapper dude did get caught in a trap and he died during the blizzard, everyone involved would be charged with murder."

"You knew that was a possibility, Melissa," Nixon said. "Maddy told you that, and I told you that."

"We would have been fine if she hadn't gotten worried about the men being trapped out there in that storm," Short said.

"Woulda, coulda, shoulda," Nixon said. "What's done is done now. I think we should call that cop and tell them the road we think Skyler is on."

"What if we go look for Skyler?" Short said. "Then he could take us to wherever Maddy is. Oh God, Rick, I'm worried about her. What if *she* dies?"

"I guess we could try, although I'm still concerned that your Subaru isn't going to make it very far if the snow is very deep."

"Let's try it. I'll be by to pick you up in twenty minutes. Do you have a gun?"

"Yes, why?"

"Because someone shot Maddy. Or we think Maddy is shot. And we might need it to protect ourselves."

Before he hung up, Short heard Nixon say something about a "shit show."

∗

Short pulled up in front of Nixon's apartment and honked the horn. A minute later, he came out the door dressed for whatever winter might throw at him. And he had a backpack on.

"What's all the gear for?" Short asked after Nixon threw the pack and a heavy coat in the back seat.

"Because who knows what we're going to run into up there," Nixon said.

"The weather forecast is for clear and sunny for the next two days," Short said. "I looked."

"There's two feet of snow, maybe more after that blizzard up there, Melissa. What if we get stuck up there too? We need to be prepared."

"I didn't think about that," Short said.

"There seems to be a lot of that going on," Nixon said snidely.

Short ignored it and turned to head back to her apartment.

"Where are we going now?"

"My place," Short said. "I'm going to get more clothes, and some food and water."

"There you go," Nixon said.

*

As they drove up the freeway, Nixon said, "You really think Maddy got shot?"

"Who else could it be?"

"Well, if Skyler was involved, who knows," Nixon said. "I guess the trapper, what's his name, Reid. It could be him."

"I thought of that, but I was thinking, if he had been shot, they probably would have left him up there."

"Now that would have been a really bad idea," Nixon said. "And who would have shot him? Who of those two even knows how to shoot a gun?"

"Maddy does. She spent some time with her daddy when he was out trapping. I'm sure he carried a gun."

Nixon didn't say anything.

"Maybe they picked up a hunter who had been shot by another hunter accidentally," Short said. "And Skyler and Maddy agreed to help them out?"

"That's a possibility, I guess. But I'd be surprised."

"Then Maddy would have the broken leg, right?" Short said.

"I don't know," Nixon said, rubbing his forehead. He was thinking that six weeks ago he hadn't known Short or any of the others, and if he hadn't been surfing the dating sites and answered

154

that post from this crazy chick, he'd be at home right now enjoying a beer and watching football.

Even though she had driven up the roads when they had scouted the trappers, Short still didn't know the roads very well. Nixon had to direct her as to where to turn and when.

"It all looks different with the snow," Short said.

Not that much different, Nixon thought, but said, "We need to go left up here."

The snow got deeper as they climbed the mountain, but there had been a few rigs up and down the road ahead of them, which made it easier for the Subaru to keep climbing.

"You think we'll be able to get all the way to Reid's trapline?" Short asked.

"I don't know," Nixon said. "We still have five miles to go."

"I sure hope Maddy is okay," Short said and kept driving up the road.

CHAPTER 23

Loots heard the vehicle coming before he saw it. He hopped off the stump and stepped into the road. He saw a white pickup coming around the bend and started to wave.

Carter was concentrating on the road, making sure not to drive off on the bend in the road and didn't see the man until the last second. His first thought was it was bigfoot. The guy was tall and wearing dark clothing. And he was waving his arms. Carter didn't want to stop, but the dude was blocking the road. As he stopped, the man who must have been pushing seven feet tall, Carter thought, walked around to the driver-side window and leaned down.

Carter rolled the window down and said, "What's up?"

"Man, am I glad to see you," Loots said. "I've been walking on this road for hours. My Jeep is stuck up the road, and I am with two injured people. My phone is dead, so I can't call for help. Can you drive me up to my Jeep?"

Carter didn't really want to get involved, but he said, "Sure, jump in."

Loots walked around the front of the pickup, climbed into the passenger seat, and said, "My name is Skyler. Thank you so much. I didn't know what I was going to do. My girlfriend—well, I guess she really isn't my girlfriend, not yet anyway—got shot, and we need to get her to the hospital."

"What?" Carter said. "Who shot her?"

"This guy who we were trying to help out of the mountains. He has a broken leg."

Carter thought about what the big man just said and couldn't make head or tails out of it.

"The guy you were helping shot your girlfriend?" Carter asked as he drove up the road.

"Yeah, and we need to get her to the hospital. She got shot yesterday, but the blizzard came in last night, so we went to this cabin that the man knew about and stayed there. I tried to drive them down in my Jeep this morning, and it got stuck."

"Did you try to stop the guy from shooting her?" Carter asked.

"Yeah, I tackled him and punched him in the face. Knocked him out. But my girlfriend didn't want to leave him there in the snow cause she thought he might die, so we took him with us. And it's a good thing we did cause he's a doctor and helped her with the gunshot wounds and he knew about the cabin where we stayed during the blizzard."

"And where did you get the guy with the broken leg?"

"That's him," Loots said. "The doctor who shot my girlfriend."

"This sounds like a soap opera," Carter said. "I'm having trouble figuring it out. Is the doctor your mother-in-law's cousin or does he have an evil twin?"

Loots thought about the question for a minute and finally said, "Geez, I don't think so."

"You're shitting me, right?" Carter said. "This didn't really happen."

"Yes, sir, it did," Loots said. "And when we get to the cabin, you will see. We have to get to the cabin so we can get Maddy to the hospital."

"Okay, okay," Carter said. "So the cabin is on this road?"

"Yes, maybe two or three miles up this road."

Carter started wondering if the cabin was the same one he had been in a couple days ago and kept driving the Chevy slowly up the road.

*

Luke was glad to see that the road to where he was going to meet Jim Simms had been driven on some since he and Austin had been on it a few hours before. There was still plenty of snow on the road, but the tire tracks made it easier to follow, and his truck did fine pulling some of the grades in four-wheel drive.

When he had driven out with Austin behind him, he had followed the snowmobile tracks down the road to an open, flat area where he could see that Simms and Matzke had loaded and unloaded their snowmobiles. When he got to that spot, the two men were parked there and were just taking the straps off the snowmachines so they could back them off the trailers.

"Gentlemen," Luke said. "Thanks for the help . . . again."

"Glad to do it," Simms said.

There was a third snowmobile on the trailer, and Matzke said, "We brought a sled for you if you want to drive it."

Luke had driven snowmobiles a time or two, and while they were amazing machines and very functional, he hadn't fallen in love with riding them.

"As long as you guys aren't going to run a hundred miles an hour," Luke said. "I'm a novice."

"We'll take it easy on ya," Simms said. "Besides, you know where you're going, so we're following you."

"Say, you didn't see some guy hiking along the road as you came up here, did you?" Luke asked, thinking they might have seen the guy who'd called in and said he was on the road.

"No, but I did see some boot tracks in the snow down a ways,"

Simms said while Matzke unloaded the third snowmobile. "Think it's that lost guy?"

"Could be, but someone might have already picked him up," Luke said.

Luke grabbed his pack out of the truck, pulled his down parka out, put it on, and threw the pack over his shoulders. Simms handed him a helmet, and Luke put it on.

"Fits just right," Luke said and put on a pair of mittens.

Luke walked over to the third snowmobile, which Matzke had idling next to his snowmachine, climbed on, and got checked out on the throttle and brakes.

Simms and Matzke climbed into snowmobile suits, pulled gloves and their helmets on, and asked Luke if he was ready.

"As John Wayne would say, 'we're burning daylight,'" Luke said and pushed the throttle, steering his sled onto the road.

They buzzed up the road, Luke leading the way at what he thought was a comfortable speed. When they approached the spur road they had all been on earlier with Austin and Jase, Luke slowed but kept running until he saw a gray Toyota Tacoma parked off the side of the road, covered in a couple feet of snow. He pulled to a stop next to the truck and turned off his snowmobile. Simms and Matzke pulled up next to him.

"This is Steve Reid's truck," Luke said as he jumped off the snowmobile and looked around the Toyota.

There were tire tracks behind the truck, but they had been snowed in.

"Someone was parked here yesterday," Luke said. "After the first snow, but before the snow last night."

"Looks like there are some footprints going up this way," Matzke said, looking down at the snow in front of Reid's pickup. "But they've been snowed in too."

The men followed the tracks in the snow a short way up the road.

"Something weird happened here," Simms said.

The men all looked and saw where the snow had been tramped down.

"It looks like someone was laying here," Luke said as he squatted for a closer look.

"Here too," Matzke said as he was pushing some of the snow out of the impression with his hands. "And I think I'm seeing some blood."

Luke moved over and looked. Then he pushed some more snow with his hands. "Yep, that's blood. And there's quite a bit of it. The guy who called in for help said one of the people he was with had been shot. My guess is this is where it happened."

"We better follow the tracks up the creek," Simms said. "Just in case Reid is still up there."

"Snowmachines would be faster," Matzke said.

"I'm not driving off-road," Luke said. "I'd hit a tree and kill myself. But I'd ride with one of you guys if you promise not to hit a tree and kill me."

Luke jumped on behind Simms, and they ran up along the small creek, staying on the snowed-in footprints. When the footprints petered out, they stopped the snowmachines and got off. Luke spotted a chain around a pine tree and knew they had found the bear trap.

"Just like Anderson said," Luke explained as he bent down and picked up the sprung bear trap. "Chain locked to a tree, running to a bear trap."

"It's hard to tell with the new snow, but my guess is Reid was caught in this one," Luke said.

"There's remnants of a small fire here," Simms said as he looked under the canopy of branches of the pine tree.

"Whoever was in that second vehicle knew Reid was up here and came and released him from the trap," Luke said. "The guy who called in that two people with him needed medical attention said one had a gunshot wound and the other had a broken leg. I bet it was Reid with the broken leg."

Simms hoisted the bear trap and said, "I wouldn't want to step into this thing. I bet it could easily break a leg."

They looked around a little more, and Matzke stepped on the folded-up marten trap under the new snow.

"Reid must have had one of these traps set here for a weasel or a mink or something," he said.

"Let's bring that back with us," Luke said. "I'd like to take the bear trap too, but we'll have to wait until we find out who has the combination to that lock."

Back at Reid's truck, they looked around some more.

"There's blood here in one of these footsteps," Simms said. "So they must have put whoever was wounded in this other vehicle but never made it to the hospital."

"The man who called in said they got stuck," Luke said. "But we would have seen a stuck vehicle on our way up here."

"Unless for some reason they were on another spur road," Simms said.

"Could be, I guess," Luke said. "If they were driving during that blizzard, it would've been very difficult to see."

"There are a couple places where a rig could drive off the road and down an embankment and we would never see it," Matzke said.

"But you would for sure see tire tracks where they went off the road," Luke said. "Even snowed- in tracks. We just weren't looking for that. Let's take it slow going down and see if we come across something like that."

Helmets on, the three men climbed on the snowmobiles and headed back down the road. Slowly.

CHAPTER 24

The Subaru was actually going pretty good in the snow. Short drove like a little old lady, Nixon thought, but better to be cautious in the snow. He almost offered to drive a couple of times but didn't want to come across as a male chauvinist. Besides, it was her car.

"You think we'll see Skyler?" Nixon asked.

"I hope so," Short said.

"Did you ever think you might be charged with murder?" he asked.

"What? No!" Short said with disgust. "Why would you even bring that up?"

"Didn't you say that cop that called was threatening you that if that trapper were to die, we'd all be charged with murder."

"He said we *could* be charged. Besides, we don't know if that has even happened."

After a while, Nixon said, "Do you think you could kill someone?"

"No!" Short said again, just as disgusted. "I hate violence of any kind. Could you?"

"I think so," Nixon said. "If I had to. Like if someone was going to kill me. I was watching the morning news, and they showed the picture of this guy who shot and killed a liquor store clerk during a robbery down in Boise. I could never do that."

"How stupid. And they have his photo? They will get him."

"The dude on the news said this guy, Travis something, is likely headed through Washington. He might be driving right by us. Wouldn't it be weird to see him like at a mini-mart or something?" Nixon said.

"There's like a one in ten million chance we'd ever see him," Short said. Then she paused and thought about it for a minute. "What would you do if you did see him?"

"He kind of looks like a little weasel, kind of rat-faced," Nixon said. "I've got my pistol. I could pull it on him and hold him until the cops came."

"Oooo, big macho man. You'd probably pee your pants," Short said. "Besides, half the killers they show on TV look like weasels to me."

"It's not like he's some kind of crazed psycho on a three-state killing spree," Nixon said. "He just shot a guy during a liquor store robbery."

"Even the crazed killers have to start somewhere," Short said. "If he did it once, he could do it again. And how do we know—maybe he already has."

"Eh, like you said. We don't need to worry about it. He's probably in Canada by now."

They talked about other things as they drove, most of the discussions involving Maddy and whether she had been shot, and if she had been shot, how it might have happened.

"I hope she's okay and we can find her," Short said one more time.

They drove up the road until they saw two trucks parked off the side of the road. One was some kind of state law enforcement truck with a badge emblem on the front doors. The other had a flat trailer attached.

"The emblem on the brown truck says Fish and Wildlife enforcement," Nixon said.

"That's who that cop who called me worked for," Short said. "His name was McClain, I think."

"You mean like the cop on *Die Hard*?" Nixon asked.

"I hate that movie," Short said. "Way too much violence for me. Bruce Willis was hot though. Does he look like a Bruce to you? I never thought he looked like a Bruce."

"Never, ever, ever thought about that," Nixon said.

"Anyway, the dude who called said he was an officer with the Department of Fish and Wildlife."

"How's someone like that involved in this?" Nixon asked. "Don't they just check people for fishing licenses and stuff?"

"I don't know," Short said. "But he sounded official to me. He was kind of menacing, frankly."

"They must be up the road on ATVs or snowmobiles," Nixon said. "See that empty trailer?"

"What should we do?" Short asked.

Nixon wanted to say, 'run like hell, don't look back, save yourself, forget about Maddy and Skyler,' but he didn't. What he did say was, "I don't think we want to be here when they come back. They've for sure been to the trapline and may have found the bear trap."

"What if the trapper is in the trap and he's dead?"

"Then we're in some serious trouble."

Short turned the Subaru around and headed back down the road.

"But what about Maddy?" she said. "I hate the thought of leaving her up here."

"Didn't the cop say Skyler said they were stuck up here someplace?" Nixon asked.

"Yeah. But we didn't see anyone stuck along the road. That purple Jeep of Skyler's would be hard to miss in all this white."

"Unless it's covered in snow," Nixon said.

Short hadn't thought about that. She just wanted to find Maddy and get her to medical help. If she could get her hands on that idiot Skyler, she'd wring his neck.

✳

Carter chatted with Skyler and learned the kid was a college student at some nearby university, but after listening to him, he wondered how he had qualified to get into college. Loots had explained a little more about how the guy who was the doctor shot his girlfriend but didn't seem to have any reason for why the doctor would start shooting at them. And Carter couldn't figure out why, after the big kid had knocked the doctor out, they didn't just get the hell out of there while he was unconscious.

"You think you could try to pull my Jeep out of that hole I backed into?" Loots asked.

"I guess I could try," Carter said. "You have a chain or tow strap?"

"Yeah, I have a strap. If we can get my Jeep out, then I can get Maddy to the hospital."

"What about the guy with the broken leg?" Carter asked.

"Yeah, he should probably get looked at too."

"Did he say how he broke his leg?" Carter asked.

Loots hesitated and then said, "Stepped into a hole, I think."

Carter had been thinking about his situation. If it was the same cabin he was headed for—and the closer they got, the more he believed it was—what was he going to do with all these extra people? If they'd been stuck up here in the mountains for the past two days, they probably hadn't heard about the man he'd shot during the liquor store robbery. So they wouldn't know he was a fugitive. But he best be prepared for it just in case.

"Have you guys been listening to the radio while you've been up here?" Carter asked.

"No, why?" Loots asked.

"Just wondered."

"You know, you never told me your name or what you're doing up this way."

"Name is Travis," Carter said. "Travis Johnson. I just wanted to see how much snow there was up here. I was driving to Seattle, but the freeway over the pass was closed, so I'm just killing time."

Loots asked where he was from and what he did, and Carter said he was from Oregon and that he was a salesman.

"You like that line of work?" Loots asked.

"It's okay," Carter said.

"I've thought I could do some kind of sales," Loots said. "I'm pretty good with people, and it would be fun meeting new people."

"Well, a lot of the people I meet are assholes," Carter said. "They all think they're better than me."

Loots didn't say anything to that. After a while, he said, "We're coming up on the turn in to the cabin. Right up here on the right."

Carter turned into the familiar, small, two-track road and went up the hill. Smoke was rolling out the chimney of the cabin, and off to the right sat the gaudiest-looking Jeep he had ever seen with its large back tires in a hole.

"Man, I'm glad to be back here," Loots said as he was getting out of the truck. "I sure hope Maddy is doing okay."

*

Reid hurt too much to get up and look out the window when he heard a vehicle pull in. He hoped it was Loots with someone who could get them down the mountain. When the woman wasn't asleep, she was calling out in pain. She needed help soon, he believed.

The cabin door opened, and in stepped Loots followed by another man.

"Skyler, thank God you're back," Haskins said. "Did you bring help?"

"Yes, this is Travis, and he's going to help pull my Jeep out,"

Loots said. "Then we can get down to the hospital."

Reid looked at Travis and wondered what he was doing up this high in the mountains. He was wearing a light red and black checked shirt, jeans, and tennis shoes. None of the clothes he was wearing were fit for the high mountains and two feet of snow.

"We're glad you made it back, Skyler, and thanks for agreeing to help out, Travis," Reid said. "Unfortunately, I'm not going to be much help. My name is Steve Reid."

Carter stepped across the small room where Reid was lying on the couch with his leg up and shook Reid's hand.

"Nice to meet you, Mr. Reid. Skyler here said you stepped in a hole and broke your leg?"

"That's not quite right," Reid said.

"And he said you shot this woman?"

"That is right," Reid said. "Long story, but I think we have it all worked out. For right now, we need to get her to the hospital. I've been treating the wound and keeping her medicated with pain relievers, but she is going to need more than I can do here."

"Skyler said you're a doctor?" Carter said.

"I was a medic in the Army," Reid said, thinking now there was no reason to lie. "Treated many wounded men in Iraq. Maddy isn't bad, but she's going to need more help than I can give, and soon."

"Please," Haskins pleaded. "We can chitchat about everything on the way to the hospital. Can you please get Skyler's Jeep unstuck so we can go?"

Loots stood up, said, "I'll grab the tow strap," and headed out the door.

Carter turned to follow Loots, and Reid saw what looked like a pistol bump in the small of the man's back.

*

The two men worked to get the strap on Loots' Jeep, and then Carter backed the Chevy around so he could pull the Jeep. Once the strap was secure on Carter's truck, he put it in low four-wheel drive and started forward. The Chevy's tires spun in the deep snow but got just enough traction to pull the Jeep up and out one foot, and then another. It was all Loots needed. As soon as his back wheels touched the ground, he was able to pull out on his own.

When Loots was clear of the hole, Carter stopped and backed up a few feet to take the tension off the strap. The men each unhooked the end of the strap attached to their vehicle. Loots threw the strap in the back of the Jeep, letting it run to warm up, and ran in to get Haskins.

Carter figured all three people would be headed down the road in Loots' Jeep, and he would have the cabin to himself. They surely wouldn't be coming back up here any time soon, and when they did, he would be long gone. He parked his truck, turned it off, and followed Loots into the cabin.

Loots almost knocked Carter out of the doorway he was moving so fast with Haskins in his arms.

"I'll get her loaded and come back for Mr. Reid," Loots said as he went by Carter.

As he was carrying Haskins to the Jeep, she said to Loots, "Listen to me. Get me in the passenger seat of the Jeep, then get in and drive us out of here."

"What about Mr. Reid," Loots said.

"Screw him. He'll be fine. We don't want to show up with him at the hospital."

"I don't under—" Loots started to say, but Haskins cut him off.

"Just do it, Skyler!" she said through gritted teeth.

And he did. He set her in the passenger seat, buckled the seatbelt around her, went around the Jeep, jumped into the driver's side, put the rig in gear, drove down the two-track driveway, and was gone.

CHAPTER 25

When they were back at their trucks, Luke hopped off the snowmobile, handed the helmet to Simms, and went to his truck.

"You guys load up and get out of here," Luke said. "You've had a long, busy day. Thanks again for everything."

He shook Simms' and Matzke's hands and turned for the truck.

"We'd be glad to help you look," Simms said.

"Just watch for tracks veering off the road," Luke said. "If you find something, call 911 when you have service and have them radio me."

"Will do," Simms said. "Be safe."

Luke drove slowly down the road, looking for anything that might tell him where the other vehicle was. If he had been five minutes sooner down the road, he would have run into Carter and Loots coming up the road in the white Chevy pickup.

*

"That's interesting," Carter said, looking out the door. "Guess they weren't happy about you shooting her. They just drove off without you."

"What?" Reid said. "I should have known."

"I'm getting a strong feeling I'm not getting the full story here, Mr. Reid, so fill me in on what I am missing."

So, Reid told him the whole story about getting his leg caught in a bear trap that those two, plus two others, had set for him, and how he'd survived one night in the trap after trying several times to get out.

"Man, that had to hurt," Carter said. "I bet you thought you were a goner."

"I even considered cutting my leg off to get out of the trap," Reid said.

"Oh, now, I couldn't do that," Carter said.

"I couldn't either. Or at least I couldn't then. I might have if it meant living or dying."

"Why did you shoot the girl?" Carter asked.

Reid told the rest of the story—how they had found him, got him out of the trap, and got him to the truck.

"But I figured out it was them who set the trap and I told them so. They didn't deny it. I had a pistol in my backpack, and when we got to my truck, I pulled the gun and told them I was going to go on my own in my rig."

"Then the big kid hit you?"

"Yeah, hit me like a linebacker and then punched me in the face. When I woke up, they had me all tied up like a Christmas goose in the back of that Jeep."

"How'd you get out of that?"

"The weather was getting really bad, the blizzard had blown in. It was next to impossible to see the road, and Skyler, the big kid, was scared. I told them about this cabin, and that I was a doctor and I could care for the girl. Which I did."

"Yeah, I was in Cle Elum when the blizzard hit. It was nasty down there. Must have been really bad up here."

"It was, but we made it through. Once the weather broke this morning, we all loaded up in the Jeep to head to the hospital, and Skyler got stuck."

"Then I found the kid down the road a few miles," Carter said. "What happened to your pistol?"

"They took it from me," Reid lied. "I don't know what they did with it."

Carter just nodded his head.

"So, what do you think we should do, Mr. Reid?"

"Can you drive me to the hospital, or if nothing else, up to my truck? I'm sure it's still sitting there. This broken leg isn't going to kill me, but I'd like to get it looked at."

About that time, they heard a vehicle drive up to the cabin.

*

Loots was driving as fast as he could down the mountain, but going downhill was probably more dangerous than up. So he was being cautious.

"Could you go a little faster, please," Haskins said.

"I could," Loots said, "but we'd probably end up plowing into a tree. Is that what you want?"

"No," she said. "I just want to get to the hospital. My insides are on fire."

"I feel pretty bad about leaving Mr. Reid up there," Loots said.

"Get over it," Haskins said. "That other guy has a truck. He can bring him down."

"I guess," Loots said and then, "Whoa! Hang on!"

Coming around the corner was a green Subaru, and there was nowhere for him to go. He applied the brakes, and somehow the Jeep stopped two inches from the grill of the other car.

"Hey," Loots said. "It's Melissa and the Prez!"

Loots got out of the Jeep, and Short and Nixon got out of the Subaru.

"Where's Maddy?" Short asked.

"Right there in my Jeep," Loots said. "She needs to get to the hospital."

"Well, get going," Short said.

"First, can you guys go up to the cabin?" Loots said. "It's only about a mile up the road on the right. You'll see our tire tracks going in and out. That trapper guy has a broken leg and needs to get to the hospital too."

"Why didn't you bring him with you?" Nixon asked.

"Because Maddy doesn't like him because he shot her," Loots said.

Short was thinking about it and finally said, "Skyler, move Maddy into my car, and Prez, you go with Loots back to the cabin to pick up the trapper. But deliver him to his house. Don't take him to the hospital. We need to figure out how we explain all of this to the cops, because as soon as a gunshot victim shows up at the emergency room, the cops will be there in five minutes."

Nixon shrugged his shoulders as if to say okay, and Loots grabbed Haskins and put her in Short's car.

"We'll talk to you guys later this evening when you get down to Ellensburg," Short said and climbed into her car.

"Bye, Maddy," Loots said. He got no response.

Both drivers struggled with turning around in the deep snow but finally made it.

As the men were driving back toward the cabin, Nixon asked, "Did Maddy ever thank you for going to get help?"

"Naw, but she is feeling pretty crappy, being gun-shot like that," Loots said.

"No excuse," Nixon said. "No excuse."

*

"I'm so sorry, Maddy," Short said. "You should've stayed home and let the guy be. He would have made it out eventually."

"No, he wouldn't have," Haskins groaned. "He would have

died, and we would all be heading to prison for murder. This was such a terrible idea."

Short didn't believe that. She still thought there was a good chance that the publicity created by all of this would sooner or later sway millions of people that trapping needed to be abolished.

"Maybe," Short said. "So what happened?"

Haskins gave her an abbreviated version because she hurt too much to talk.

"He knew it was you . . . us . . . who set the trap up there?"

"He's not stupid, Melissa. Yes, he figured it out pretty quickly. And he thought we were going to kill him because he was going to call the cops on us."

"Did he know about me and the Prez?"

"After that dolt Skyler told him, he did," Haskins said. "I swear, for as big as Skyler is, he must have a brain the size of a tennis ball."

"His heart is in the right place," Short said. "The cops were going to figure it out anyway. The one who called me knew I was involved somehow."

"You got a call from a cop?"

"Yeah, when I couldn't get ahold of you or Skyler, I figured you had come up here to check the traps, so I called in a missing person's report on you. The cop, he said he was with Fish and Wildlife, called, and somehow he had put two and two together."

"Fish and Wildlife don't have cops, do they?" Haskins said. "And why would they care anyway?"

"I guess trapping bears is against the law, and bears are wildlife," Short said.

"But we weren't trapping bears."

"Yeah, he figured that out right away, I think. He was looking for the trapper, the guy who shot you, because they also had a missing person's report on him."

Haskins just groaned.

"I'm hurrying," Short said.

"Skyler drives like a ninety-year-old man," Haskins said. "I'm glad you are taking me to the hospital."

"These roads are terrible," Short said. "I'll get there as quickly as I can."

*

Luke was moving down the road at a snail's pace. There had to be some kind of tracks in the snow along the road. He believed he was missing something.

He radioed in to dispatch and asked them to call the local hospital in Ellensburg to see if they had anyone there with a gunshot wound, or if Steve Reid was there to have a broken leg attended to. He wasn't positive it was Reid who had the broken leg, but someone had been in that bear trap, and it made sense that it had been Reid.

Three minutes later, the voice on the radio said there were no recent gunshot victims, and nobody named Reid had been to the hospital.

That meant the person with the gunshot wound and Reid were most likely still up here somewhere, Luke thought.

It was getting darker, and Luke decided he would make one more pass up the road to Reid's pickup. If he didn't find anyone walking or driving, he would call it a day. It seemed like it had been three days since he and the boys had been in the culvert during the blizzard, but that was just twenty-four hours ago. He was starting to run out of juice.

Luke found a place to turn around, pulled off the road, and sat for a minute. He was hungry and thirsty, so he pulled a granola bar and a bottle of water out of his pack. As he ate, he was thinking about how he was looking forward to being home in his bed when his radio crackled again.

"Wildlife 148."

"Wildlife 148," Luke said. "Go ahead."

"We had a call a couple minutes ago from a man named Sam Anderson. He tried to call you and wasn't able to get through. He said he had another thought about the missing trapper. Evidently, there is a small cabin up there not far from where he told you Steve

Reid may have his trapline. He's only used it once, but he knows Reid uses it often."

"Roger," Luke said. "Did he give you any GPS coordinates?"

"No, but I could call him back and get them for you."

"That would be great," Luke said.

As he was sitting there, he saw a green Subaru come around the bend and continue down the road. He watched through his rearview mirror as the car went by. A woman was driving, and it didn't look like anyone else was in the car.

"Here are the coordinates," the dispatcher said and gave them to Luke.

He jotted them down on a pad on his console and thought about the Subaru that had just gone by. He didn't get the license number but still called it in.

"One more thing," Luke said as he looked at the notes he had taken during his conversation with the woman about the missing person call she had placed. He found her name and said, "Can you find a vehicle registration for a Melissa Short? No street address, but I know she lives in Ellensburg."

"Stand by," the dispatcher said.

A moment later, the dispatcher reported that the car registered to Melissa Short was a 2014 Subaru Outback, Washington license plate EGP117. Color green.

Luke thanked the dispatcher. That had to be Short.

Now he had a dilemma. Should he catch up to the green Subaru or go check out the cabin? He decided to go to the cabin. That had to be where Reid was. He could always stop at Short's place of residence on the way through Ellensburg later.

CHAPTER 26

"Looks like they came back for you," Carter said after looking out the window and seeing the bright purple Jeep pulling up in front of the cabin. He had just lit the gas lantern and thrown another couple of chunks of wood in the fireplace.

"Good. That way I won't need to bother you to drive me all the way back to Ellensburg," Reid said.

Carter had told Reid the same story he'd told Loots. He said he was on his way to Seattle and got delayed by the closure of the interstate.

As they pulled in, Nixon looked at the white Chevy pickup parked in front of the cabin and noticed it had an Idaho license plate. That sparked something in his memory. He was pretty sure the TV news person this morning had said the guy who'd killed the liquor store clerk in Boise might be driving a white Chevy pickup. He watched Loots hop out of the Jeep and then he climbed out. He checked the pistol tucked into the back of his pants.

"What happened?" Carter asked as Loots came through the front door. The big guy was followed by a man with a scraggly beard and long, dark, greasy hair. He might be homeless, Carter thought.

"We ran into some friends," Loots said. "We sent Maddy with one of them to the hospital, and we came back to get Mr. Reid."

Carter noticed that the homeless guy was looking at him.

"Thank you," Reid said. "Now, Mr. Johnson here can get back to the freeway and on his way to Seattle."

*

Nixon recognized Carter immediately. And, as he looked at the fugitive, he was pretty sure that Carter saw that he recognized him. He needed to do something quick.

He walked toward Carter, stuck out his hand, and said, "I'm Rick Nixon. Have we met before?"

Carter shook his hand and said, "I don't think so. Travis Johnson is my name."

Not the name of the fugitive, Nixon thought. Definitely could be a fake name though.

"Where'd you go to high school?" Nixon asked, looking at the face of the man. Yep, it was the guy from the TV story. It was the same weaselly face. "I know I know you. Maybe from high school?"

"I went to high school in Portland," Carter said. "You don't look familiar to me."

Nixon smiled and shook his head. "I'll figure it out."

Nixon hoped he had sold it and it was going to be good enough to slow the fugitive down. He'd told Melissa he would pull the gun and call the cops if he did happen to run into the killer. Now he wasn't sure what to do. He figured there was a better-than-ninety-percent chance that Johnson, or whatever his real name was, was packing a pistol.

"Okay, Mr. Reid, are you ready to hit the road?" Loots asked. "Prez and I will get you out of here and down to the hospital."

"Not so quick," Carter said as he pulled his pistol.

"What's going on?" Reid asked.

"I'm going to need your keys, big guy," Carter said to Loots, pointing his pistol at him.

Loots looked stupefied, which wasn't much different from his regular look.

"But we have to take Mr. Reid to the hospital," Loots said.

"He'll be fine," Carter said. "Now, I'm going to need all of you to lay face down on the floor. You too," he said to Reid.

Reid slowly worked his way off the couch and thought about the gun in his belt. If he lay face down, the man would see it for sure.

Nixon was thinking the exact same thing. Was there anything he could do or say to get the killer's attention just long enough that he could get his pistol out of his pants? He had never practiced pulling the pistol from his back and frankly didn't know if he could even hit anything. But if this guy intended to lay them down and shoot them in the back of the head, well, he needed to do something.

Reid, on the other hand, had practiced pulling his pistol many times. Not in case he was caught in a holdup or whatever this was, but because he'd been tracked two different times by cougars while he walked his traplines. If a cougar was going to charge, he wanted to be ready. And Reid had practiced with his pistol. He could hit the bullseye nine times out of ten at twenty yards at the range. He had the same thoughts as Nixon. If this guy meant to do them harm, Reid was going to give him a fight.

"Right now!" Carter barked. "And the keys! I need your keys!"

"Can't you just take your truck?" Loots said, not grasping the situation.

It looked like Carter was going to shoot the big guy when they all heard a rig pulling in.

∗

Luke watched his GPS and followed the road back up the hill. When he got close to where the cabin was based on the coordinates, he looked around and didn't see anything. There was just a wall of trees and snow. Then he looked closer. Tire tracks ran off the road to the right and disappeared up a narrow, two-track road through the trees. He couldn't believe he hadn't noticed it before.

When he got through the trees, he saw a small cabin with two rigs sitting in front of it. A purple Jeep with huge tires. And a white pickup. Gray smoke was curling out of the cabin's chimney.

This had to be where Reid was, he thought. He climbed out of the truck and headed for the door.

*

Carter, while still holding the gun on the three men, took a quick peek out the window. Another guy was walking up to the door.

"Don't say a word," Carter hissed. "Or I'll kill you all."

There was a knock on the door, and Carter, as he was moving his gun hand behind his back, said, "C'mon in."

He couldn't believe it when the guy coming through the door had a badge emblem on his coat.

"Hi, fellas," Luke said, quickly assessing the situation. Everyone looked nervous, and the one guy had his hand behind his back. Another was holding a leg up and looked like he'd been in a fight with an alligator.

"Mr. Reid," Luke said, looking at the man with the hurt leg, "We've been looking for you."

"You've found me," Reid said and shifted his eyes quickly toward Carter.

Luke noticed the glance toward the man with his hand behind his back. "I'm Luke McCain. I'm a state police officer. I need to see all your IDs, please."

"That won't be necessary," Carter said, pulling the gun out from behind his back.

Luke moved his hand toward his pistol, and Carter pointed his gun at him and said, "I wouldn't do that."

Then he ordered Luke to stand with the other men as he moved in a half-circle toward the door.

"Let's try this again, dufus," Carter said to Loots. "I need your keys." Then he turned to Luke and said, "Yours too."

"Mine are still in my truck," Luke said. "So what is this all about?"

Carter didn't say anything. Luke could see the guy was agitated. Maybe he needed drugs. But why was he up here in the middle of this whole trapping situation?

"You don't know who I am, do you?" Carter finally said.

"I have no clue who you are," Luke said. "I've been up here in the woods for the past three days looking for all these people, so if I'm supposed to know you, I'm sorry. But if you want the keys to the rigs, take them and get on your way."

Carter thought about that. He believed the cop. But the homeless guy knew who he was and what he had done. He was sure of it.

"Give me your pistol," Carter said to Luke.

"Yeah, I'm not supposed to do that," Luke said. "My boss will be pissed, and I'll get in trouble. How 'bout I just keep it holstered, and you go get in whichever rig you want and move on."

"That ain't happenin' without your pistol," Carter said.

Carter was flustered. He didn't think he could kill the four men without one of them jumping him. They were just too close in the little cabin. And if he shot a state police officer, every cop in the country would want to hunt him down and hang his ass from the highest tree. There would be no chance to get away. He really didn't want a hostage, but if he took the homeless guy, then he wouldn't be able to tell the others who Carter was and what he had done. Maybe that would give him a little more time to get away.

"I won't shoot you, I promise," Luke said. "Go on if you're going."

"You!" Carter said pointing his pistol at Nixon. "You're coming with me."

Nixon started shaking his head. "What do you want me for?"

"I'll shoot you right here, I swear to God. Now, c'mon!"

Luke gave Nixon a look that said it would be okay and said, "Go ahead. It'll be alright."

Nixon started toward the door, and Luke saw that the man had a handgun stuck in his belt in the back of his pants. This wasn't good. Someone was going to get killed.

"Wait a second," Luke said. "Maybe you should take me."

"Bullshit," Carter said. "Get over here and let's get going," he said to Nixon.

Nixon started toward the door again, and just then Reid screamed and fell to the floor. Everyone turned that way and then, BOOM! BOOM! BOOM!

CHAPTER 27

It took a little bit to unravel what had just happened. Luke's ears were still ringing from the shots, and dust was swirling around through the dim light of the gas lantern and the fireplace.

At the sound of the first shot, Luke had pulled his pistol while he was dropping to the floor. He'd seen the guy with the gun go down like he'd been shot, and the guy with the long hair go down too.

Luke looked around at the other men. Reid was down, and the big guy with the blond hair was just standing there.

Luke stood up, keeping his pistol on the gunman. He walked four steps to the man and saw he'd been shot right through the throat. The man's eyes were open, but he was long gone. Probably was dead before his body hit the floor. Still, Luke kicked his pistol away.

Next, Luke moved to the guy with the long hair. He could see he was still breathing. In fact, as Luke got there, he started moaning.

"I'm shot," Nixon said. "I'm shot."

Luke kneeled next to the man and saw another pistol lying next to him. He kicked that pistol away too and turned to Loots and Reid.

"You guys okay?" Luke asked.

"You'll probably want this," Reid said, holding a pistol up by the barrel to give to Luke.

Then it dawned on Luke that Reid had shot someone, most likely the man who was holding the gun on everyone.

"Can you help your friend?" Luke said to Loots. "Don't move him, but find out where he has been shot."

"I didn't shoot him," Reid said. "Just that asshole that was going to kill us. He was going to lay us on our stomachs, and I think he was going to kill us. But you pulled in just in time."

"Do you know who he was or what he wanted?" Luke asked.

"I do," came a moaning voice by the door.

"He's shot in the butt," Loots said. "Blood's coming from a bullet hole in his butt."

"What's your name?" Luke asked Nixon.

"Rick Nixon," Nixon groaned. "That guy is a fugitive from Idaho. I saw his photo on TV this morning. He shot some liquor store clerk during a holdup a couple of days ago."

"What the hell is he doing up here?" Reid asked.

"Who knows," Luke said. "And I guess we never will."

"Is he dead?" Loots asked. "Ah geez. The girls told me no one was going to die."

"And what is your name?" Luke asked.

"Skyler Loots, sir," Loots said. "Boy, am I glad you showed up when you did. I think Mr. Reid is right. I thought that guy was going to kill us, like you see on those gangster movies. I was going to try to tackle him, like I did with Mr. Reid, but I didn't have to."

"It's okay," Luke said. "So were you the guy who called in to the sheriff's department that you were lost up here?"

"Yeah, I—"

"Hey, I'm shot and bleeding here," Nixon interrupted with a loud moan.

"I was a medic in the Army," Reid said to Luke. "If we can get some better light on his wound, I can at least stop the bleeding. Skyler, get me the red bag."

Loots got the bag, and then he and Luke helped Nixon to the bed, laying him down on his stomach. They undid his pants and slid them down, revealing a white derrière with a deep slash running down at an angle across his right cheek.

"Just a flesh wound," Reid said. "You might need some stitches, but you'll be fine."

Looking at the wound, Luke thought he knew what had happened. When Reid shot Carter, Nixon tried to pull his pistol and shot himself in the butt. But he was positive he'd heard three shots. He went over to the pistol he'd kicked away from Carter, knelt down, and smelled it. Definitely recently fired. He stood up and started looking around. The light was too crappy to see much, but there had to be a bullet stuck somewhere, either in the wall or roof of the cabin from Carter's gun.

"Skyler, you help Mr. Reid attend to Mr. Nixon here, and I'm going to go out and call this in. I don't know if we can get an ambulance up this high with the snow so deep, but we'll get you out of here as soon as we can."

"What's another hour or two," Reid said sarcastically.

"Speak for yourself," Nixon groaned. Then he said, "Say, officer, can we say that the bad guy shot me? I'd be a hero in some of my classes for getting hit."

"We need to talk about several things," Luke said. "Let me get help on the way."

As he was walking out the door, Luke heard Loots say, "Are we sure that Mr. Johnson is really dead?"

"His name wasn't Johnson," Nixon groaned. "That was an alias."

"An alias?" Loots asked.

"Yes, an alias, and yes, he is dead thanks to Mr. Reid."

*

It took seventy-five minutes for the first of the Kittitas County deputies to arrive. Luke recognized Alivia Hernandez immediately. The short, stocky, black-haired deputy was riding with another officer named Kurtz, who Luke had never met before.

"There you go again," Hernandez said after she walked up from the KCSD four-wheel-drive SUV. "Running down another killer. Where are the TV cameras?"

Luke ignored her comments and said, "Good to see you, Hernandez. Hope I didn't drag you away from your important work with all those four-legged criminals."

"Hey," she said. "That dog almost bit me. I thought I was going to have to shoot it! Speaking of which, did you shoot the dead guy in the cabin?"

"No, another man did. Possibly saved our lives."

"We ran the name you gave us," Hernandez said. "He was wanted for murder in Boise. Evidently, he jacked up a liquor store and shot the cashier who tried to pull a gun on him."

"That's what one of the other guys said," Luke said as they walked into the cabin.

Hernandez walked around Carter's body, and as soon as Nixon saw her come through the door, he said, "Could someone cover my ass, please?"

"How did the homeless guy get shot?" Hernandez asked in a whisper.

"I'll tell you later," Luke whispered back.

Luke gave her a quick rundown on what happened in the shootout, and she stepped over to Reid.

"Good shooting, sir."

"I wasn't in the mood to be sitting in this cabin much longer," Reid said. "But here I am, still sitting here."

"We'll get you on the road to the hospital shortly," Hernandez said.

Two other KCSD rigs showed up ten minutes later, and Reid and Nixon were loaded into one of them.

"They'll take you to an ambulance waiting down on the plowed part of the road," Hernandez said after the two were in the SUV. Then she pounded on the side of the rig, sending them on their way.

"Was I right about a wounded girl showing up at the hospital?" Luke asked.

When he'd called in the report of the shooting, he told the dispatcher to have someone watching for a green Subaru to show up at the emergency room with Melissa Short.

"Yep, Ellensburg PD was waiting for them. The wounded girl is in the ER. Sounds like she might need some surgery to make sure to stop any infection. The other girl is on her way to the Kittitas County jail."

Loots overheard them talking and said, "Is Maddy going to be okay?"

"Sounds like it," Luke said. "Might need some surgery, but she should be fine."

"That's good," Loots said. "She can be kinda bossy, but I still like her."

Luke didn't have the heart to tell him that they all might be spending some time in jail. Although if the big guy got a good lawyer, he might be able to get away with the "I just did what I was told" defense. And if Loots was put on the stand, the jury would certainly believe it, Luke thought.

The Kittitas County coroner showed up twenty minutes later and started doing his thing. He had a minion with him who set up lights powered by some kind of high-tech lithium batteries so the coroner could see inside the cabin.

Luke walked through the shooting again for the coroner, step by step. Finally, the coroner looked closely at Carter's body, and then he and the minion placed it in a body bag and put it on a gurney. They should have put it on a sled because the gurney didn't move in the deep snow when they tried to roll it out of the cabin.

Because of the bad roads, the coroner-mobile couldn't get up to the cabin, so they carried Carter's body and put it in the bed of Luke's pickup.

"Going to be a cold ride," Hernandez said.

"I don't think he's going to mind," Luke said.

Finally, the coroner said he had seen all he needed to see, and everyone started migrating to their rigs.

Loots was headed to his Jeep, and Luke caught up with him.

"You seem like a nice guy, Skyler, but we're going to have to talk sometime soon about this whole deal with you guys setting those bear traps."

"Yeah, that was pretty stupid, wasn't it?"

"Not very smart," Luke said. "And illegal. Frankly, I could arrest you right now, but I don't want to do that. Just stick around, okay? We'll figure it out tomorrow or the next day."

Loots said he wasn't going anywhere except to the hospital to check on Haskins.

Hernandez walked over as Luke was getting into his truck. "I just heard from the sergeant that the TV stations, including one from Seattle, are calling. He said some may be waiting in Cle Elum to get some footage and the story."

"You are going to look great on TV, Hernandez," Luke said.

"Oh, no. You're the TV star."

"Not this time," Luke said. "I have to deliver Carter's body to the morgue. No stopping for anything. Direct orders from the coroner himself."

"Ah, crap," Hernandez said.

"Maybe they'll ask you about the stud you had to arrest," Luke said with a smile.

"It was a stallion," she said. Then she added, "Ass." But Luke could see her smiling.

Luke jumped into his truck and fired it up. As he was pulling out, he rolled his window down and said, "I'll be watching for you on the morning news!"

Then he quickly rolled the window up, looked in his side mirror, and saw Hernandez yelling something at him but couldn't hear a word she was saying.

As he drove, Luke thought about everything that had transpired over the past two days. No wonder he was tired. It felt like he'd walked a hundred miles in knee-deep snow, had driven even more miles, and then he'd come who-knows-how-close to being shot. He never did see where Carter's bullet ended up, but it could have just as easily hit him.

He was tired, and as he thought about it, he was hungry too. He didn't care that the coroner had ordered him to go directly to the morgue. A guy had to eat, so he stopped at a little sub sandwich shop in Ellensburg he knew stayed open late for the university students and ordered a ten-inch honey mustard chicken with bacon on wheat and an extra-large Pepsi to wash it down. He was going to need all the caffeine he could get for the drive home.

As he waited for the sandwich, he called Sara.

"How you doing?" she asked.

"Okay," he said. "Long few days. I just need to be home for a while. I need some sleep and I need to see you."

The thought of possibly catching a bullet brought things into focus. He really appreciated the important things in his life. He was so tired he decided not to give Sara the full story right now. Instead, he just said that they had rounded up all the bad guys and girls and now he was headed home. She'd get the blow-by-blow account later.

"Did you call Bob?" she asked.

"No, it can wait until tomorrow."

"Okay," she said. "I'll wait up. Looking forward to seeing you too."

CHAPTER 28

When Luke woke up the next morning, he opened one eye and what did he see? A yellow dog sitting next to the bed with his face about five inches from Luke's.

"Hey, Jack," Luke said. "Are you mad that I had Austin bring you home?"

The dog didn't say anything, he just stared.

Luke could smell bacon frying in the kitchen. He looked at the digital clock on the nightstand. It read 10:27. He hadn't slept that late since, well, he couldn't remember when. He got up, pulled on some sweatpants and a W.S.U. sweatshirt, and stumbled out to the kitchen.

"That smells good," Luke said.

Sara was standing in front of the stove. She had on green sweatpants and a University of Oregon sweatshirt. Luke had thought about making those disappear sometime when Sara was away at work, but she was an FBI agent and would have figured out what had happened, and then he would have been in BIG trouble. So Luke stomached having to look at the attire. The only thing that made the picture palatable was that his beautiful wife was in the outfit.

"I sent Jack in to wake you up," she said. "I thought you might sleep until noon."

"I think I could have," Luke said. "But I better be checking in with the captain. Hey, why aren't you at work?"

"I told them I was taking some comp time this morning," she said. "There was nothing going on at the office today anyway."

Luke walked up behind her and wrapped his arms around her. "I do love you," he said softly into her ear.

Sara turned around and kissed him. "Enough, or I'll burn the bacon. Grab a plate. The eggs and toast will be ready in a minute."

During breakfast he told her the whole story about finally finding Reid and getting tangled up with the fugitive from Idaho. He left out the part about Carter shooting somewhere close to him.

"That Reid must be a good shot," Sara said.

"He said he practices with the pistol all the time," Luke said. "It's possible he saved a life or two."

"Well, I hope they don't go easy on those kids who set the traps," Sara said. "I saw that Deputy Hernandez on the news this morning. She said it was a Department of Fish and Wildlife officer who caught the bad guys. Didn't mention you by name."

"Atta girl. I owe her one. Hey, I noticed the walk and the drive were shoveled," Luke said as he was putting his dishes in the dishwasher.

"Austin did it," Sara said. "Said it was a thank you for coming up there and finding him and Jase."

"That was nice of him," Luke said. "Since it's your day off, you might have had to get out there and do it."

She gave him one of her looks.

"Not that I wouldn't have been out there with you. That was a fantastic breakfast by the way," Luke said, changing the subject.

"Thank you so much!"

Didn't work. She was still giving him the look.

"Okay, well, I need to go call the captain," Luke said and headed for his cell phone.

Davis was glad to hear from Luke. The captain already had received a briefing on what happened from the Kittitas County sheriff.

"The sheriff says thanks, by the way," Davis said. "They're getting the credit for catching that Carter guy."

"That's fine with me," Luke said. "It was kind of incidental to the missing trapper situation. I'm just glad that it turned out as well as it did. Steve Reid could have easily been out there for days. Although after talking with Sam Anderson, I think we would have gotten to him last night."

"Well, it was good work," Davis said. "Now for the bad news. We have at least four different elk hunters still stuck up in the mountains. If you're up to it, we could really use some more help."

Luke had kind of forgotten about that. With two major snowstorms back-to-back, he was surprised there were only four hunters still out there.

"Let me get a shower and replenish my backpack," Luke said.

"I'll have Hargraves meet you at one o'clock at the café in Naches," Davis said. "He's coordinating with the Yakima Search and Rescue."

"10-4," Luke said and clicked off.

"No rest for the weary?" Sara asked.

"I guess not. There are still some hunters either missing or stuck up in the mountains, and Search and Rescue needs whatever help they can get."

*

Two hours later, Luke was pulling in to the café in Naches. Hargraves' rig was already parked in front of the place. Luke got out of his truck, told Jack who was sound asleep on the back seat that he would only be a minute, and headed into the restaurant.

He found Hargraves sitting with Jim Kingsbury and Frank Dugdale. The two men, gray-haired in their sixties, were local characters. They liked to fish and hunt and, like a couple of old ladies, they knew all the gossip about what was going on around town.

All three men at the table were eating hot turkey sandwiches. Luke took a quick glance to see what shirt Kingsbury had on. The man was famous for wearing a t-shirt with a different political comment or funny saying on it every day. Today's shirt was gray with black lettering that read "IF I AGREED WITH YOU THEN WE'D BOTH BE WRONG."

"Sit down and join us," Dugdale, the man with three first names, said. "We were just hearing about your shootout up there above Cle Elum last night."

"Hargraves here didn't have all the particulars," Kingsbury said. "It'll be good to get it from the horse's mouth."

"Nice shirt, by the way," Luke said to Kingsbury and then to Hargraves, "I'm not sure we have time."

He gave Hargraves a look like maybe they should get going.

"Let me finish my lunch," Hargraves said as he mopped up some white gravy with a piece of bread. "It's pretty good. You should try it."

"It's the special today," Dugdale said. "Hot turkey sandwich with all the fixings for nine bucks."

"I had a big breakfast just a little bit ago, but I might have a piece of pie," Luke said.

When the waitress came by a minute later, Luke ordered a piece of raspberry-rhubarb pie, heated with a scoop of ice cream, and then went on to tell the story of the shootout to the men.

"Where did the bullet go from the Idaho guy's gun?" Kingsbury asked. "Sounds like it could have hit you or the big kid standing there."

"Not sure," Luke said. "I'm guessing the sheriff's investigator will find it. Probably in the floor."

"Weren't you on the floor?" Dugdale asked.

"Yes, I was."

Hargraves, Kingsbury, and Dugdale all took a bite of turkey, chewed, and thought about that for a minute.

"So, where we headed?" Luke asked Hargraves, changing the subject.

"We're going to meet the deputy coordinating with Search and Rescue up at the landing strip at Rimrock. They've got a helicopter there that has already located a couple of camps that are snowed in."

"There are probably more," Luke said.

"I'm sure there are. The captain said he's gotten a couple dozen calls."

The men chatted about lost hunters, and the discussion came back around to the people who were setting traps to catch trappers.

"You really think they thought this thing through?" Kingsbury asked. "They don't like violence, yet they use it to try to get people on their side."

"I haven't really had a chance to talk with any of them about it other than the big guy, Loots is his name. He decided after the fact that it was probably a pretty stupid thing to do."

"No kidding," Hargraves said.

"But I got the impression he had a thing for the girl who got shot and was just doing what she told him to do. He told me that she was pretty bossy."

"Women," Dugdale said.

"What do you know of women?" Kingsbury asked. "You haven't even been around one in twenty-five years."

"There is a reason for that," Dugdale said. "And what about you?"

Kingsbury made a funny face and did a backhanded wave, like he was just waving his friend's comment away.

"Well, it's a good thing you guys have each other," Luke said, then to Hargraves, "Should we roll?"

Hargraves threw a twenty on the table, and they headed for the door.

CHAPTER 29

The landing strip at Rimrock Lake was a beehive of activity when Luke and Hargraves arrived. Snowmobiles were buzzing around, and side-by-sides were pulling in while others were pulling out. Luke could see a group of three guys just standing there watching. They were hunters, Luke decided, who had just been brought to the landing strip, either by ground or by air.

Luke parked next to Hargraves and got out to go find the officer in charge of the operation.

"Hey, Luke," came a call from a group of men and women standing near a big tent.

Luke looked and saw Bob Williams, a sergeant with the Yakima County Sheriff's Office waving at him. Normally, Williams would call Luke 'Rifleman' because the main character from that 1960s television show *The Rifleman* was named Lucas McCain. Today, the sergeant had a serious look on his face.

"What's up?" Luke asked when he got to Williams.

"Something has just popped up. The helicopter spotted something up on Pinegrass Ridge. We think it might be a husband and wife. We had a call from a woman after the first big snow the day before yesterday who said she was with her husband hunting above Rimrock Lake somewhere. They were trying to hike out, and the blizzard was about to hit, so they took cover in a small cave. The snow covered the entrance, and her husband had what she thinks is a heart attack while trying to dig out. He's alive, she said, but she thinks he shouldn't walk. She was able to finally dig out and call for help, but her phone went dead as the 911 operator was talking to her. We've been searching from the air, and the chopper pilot just found a spot where someone had spelled out H-E-L-P in the snow."

"Okay, what do you need me to do?"

"The chopper can't land anywhere close to the spot, but they'd be able to get you a half-mile or so away. If they took you and Jack in there, you think you could find them?"

"Probably," Luke said. "What about the snowmachines? Can't they get there?"

"Too steep," Williams said. "In this snow, they can't get to where the pilot saw the SOS."

"Let me get ready," Luke said and headed back to his truck.

"Want me to go with you?" Hargraves asked.

"No, we've got it," Luke said.

Luke grabbed his pack, snowshoes and walking poles and then called Jack. "C'mon, boy. Time to go to work."

Luke heard the helicopter before he saw it. A minute later, the black chopper came down the lake and landed on the strip, sending dry snow flying everywhere.

Jack had never been in a helicopter before, but Luke felt the dog would do just fine. He had flown in airplanes twice and never seemed apprehensive about it.

When they got the sign from the pilot, Luke had Jack heel, and the two went as quickly as they could to the chopper, Luke ducking his head even though the blades were rotating a good twelve feet above him. They went to an open side door, Luke threw his gear in, and then he bent down and picked Jack up and set him in.

"Luke McCain," Luke yelled over to the pilot. "And this is Jack."

"Hank Pierce," the pilot said, handing Luke some headphones. "Buckle up, and we'll be on our way."

Luke buckled his seatbelt, put the headphones on, and a second later a voice crackled in the earpieces. It was Pierce. Luke saw his mouth moving and heard him say, "We'll be to the landing area in five minutes."

They lifted off, and Luke watched the people at the tent go from actual size to tiny specks in just a few seconds.

"I'll drop you at the spot, and if you find the people, radio in," Pierce said. "If you can get them to the landing spot, that would be best. If not, I'll have to call another helicopter to get a basket down for them to be lifted out. I'm not equipped to do that."

"Roger," Luke said.

He watched the country below and tried to get himself acclimated. He'd spent hundreds of hours patrolling this area, but it all looked a little different from five thousand feet.

When they were over the help sign spelled out in the snow, Pierce slowed the chopper and hovered.

"We'll be landing due south about a half mile," Pierce said.

Thirty seconds later, the helicopter slowed again and started to drop. Luke looked at Jack who was calmly lying at his feet. As soon as the tires bumped ground, Pierce said, "Here you go."

Luke said, "Thanks for the lift. See you soon I hope," and he and Jack jumped out of the chopper. Luke grabbed his gear, ducked down, and walked out from under the swirling blades.

Pierce gave Luke a thumbs up, and a minute later the helicopter was nothing more than a dark spot in the sky.

Luke put his snowshoes on while Jack sniffed around a bit. The snow was up to the dog's belly, so he was having to jump through the snow to get anywhere.

Snowshoes and backpack on, Luke grabbed the poles and started toward where the request for help had been spelled in the snow.

After a minute, Jack fell in behind Luke, and the two of them trudged through the snow.

*

They'd been walking along the ridge for almost a half hour when Luke found the wood and fir branches that had been used to spell the word help. Small tracks were all over the place, coming and going in several different directions, obviously made by the person hunting for materials to build the word and bring them back to the spot.

"Okay, boy," Luke said. "We need to find these folks quickly."

Jack already had his nose in the air and was moving to the northeast. There were foot tracks going that way, Luke could see, so he hoped Jack scented the people. He followed the tracks almost perfectly, although he wasn't sniffing the tracks. He was air-scenting something or someone, Luke knew.

"Good dog," Luke said as encouragement.

They worked toward some big white humps that looked like giant scoops of ice cream, which Luke knew were big boulders covered in two feet of snow. The tracks went right toward the rocks, and so did Jack.

In two minutes, Jack stopped down the hill below one very large boulder and started digging in the snow. A second later, Luke heard a woman's voice yelling, "Help! Help!"

Jack's digging pushed through the snow, and in another minute Luke could see an arm reaching out of the widening hole.

"Good dog," Luke said again and moved in to push more snow away. As he did, he could see two people together in a small cave under the overhang of one of the boulders. It looked like many of the bear dens Luke had seen over the years.

"Thank God, you're here," the woman said. "My husband is sick. I thought we were going to die together out here."

"My name is Luke, and this is my dog, Jack. We're going to get you out of here as quickly as we can."

"Thank you so much," the woman said. "I'm Heather Robbins, by the way, and this is my husband, Mike."

"How'd you find this place?" Luke asked.

"Just lucky, I guess. It was starting to snow and blow, and Mike knew we needed to find some kind of shelter." Then she pointed and said, "Look."

Luke looked over to the wall of the little cave and saw some faded red drawings of a stick figure man with a spear in his hand aiming at a stick figure deer. A red sun was nearby.

"Native pictographs," he said. "Looks like you aren't the first people to ever stay here."

"I think their spirits were with us. Mike was trying to build a door with the snow to close us in, and I think he had a heart attack. But he didn't die."

"Do you need anything?" Luke asked. "Water or food?"

"No, we're fine. We always carry what we need to stay in the wild for a couple days if we were to get lost."

Luke could see where they had built a small fire. And they both were dressed in good coats, pants, and boots.

"Okay," Luke said. "Here is what we are going to do. I'll go out and radio the Search and Rescue folks that we have found each other, and then we'll figure out how to either get you and Mike to a pick-up point or get a helicopter that can drop a basket and pick you up."

"I think I can walk a ways," Mike said. "Heather is just a worrier."

As he was loading into the helicopter at the landing strip, Williams had given Luke a handheld radio already tuned in to the frequency they were using, so Luke turned it on and told whoever answered what their situation was.

"We're going to try to walk to the drop point," Luke said. "I'll stay in touch and let you know how we're doing."

Luke gave his snowshoes to Mike who did better walking

than Luke had expected. Heather Robbins did just fine too. They trudged through the deep snow at a slow but steady pace. Luke guessed they were in their fifties, both in excellent shape.

When they were almost to the pick-up spot, Luke radioed in, and five minutes later they heard the chopper coming. As the helicopter was landing, all three people and one yellow dog made their way over to the aircraft. Luke helped Mr. and Mrs. Robbins climb in.

"Welcome aboard," Pierce said to the couple. Then to Luke, he said, "I'll have to come back and get you. I can only fly two passengers at a time."

"No problem," Luke said. "See you in a few."

Luke again watched as the helicopter vanished in the distance. Then he walked over to a big fir tree seventy yards away, the late afternoon sun shining on its trunk. He pulled a small plastic tarp out of his pack, unfolded it on the snow, and sat down with his back against the tree.

His eyes had only been closed a few seconds when the radio crackled again.

"Hey, Rifleman," Williams said. "Looks like your ride back is going to be a while. They decided to take Mr. Robbins directly to the hospital in the helicopter. Hope you don't mind."

"Not at all," he said into the radio and shut his eyes.

The warm sun was hitting him in the face, and Jack was lying next to him.

"Not at all," he mumbled to himself.

*

Three weeks after the shootout at the cabin, Luke was at an arraignment hearing at the courthouse in Ellensburg. Short, Haskins, Loots, and Nixon had all been arrested on a list of things including aggravated assault, among others.

Short, who Luke hadn't seen up close until then, showed absolutely no remorse for her part in the setting of the bear traps and was later sentenced to two months in jail. The others received no jail time, as the judge took into account that Loots and Haskins had gone up to save Steve Reid. Plus, with Haskins' and Nixon's gunshot wounds, the judge figured they had paid enough for their crimes.

The prosecutor decided there was no reason to charge Reid with any crimes for shooting Haskins or Carter. Both shootings, he believed, were justifiable.

The shootings made the news around the Northwest, mostly because the Washington authorities had somehow tracked down Carter after he had gotten away with ten thousand dollars from a liquor store in Boise after killing the cashier at the store. No one knew what Carter had done with the cash because when the police checked his body and his truck, they only found a little over eleven hundred dollars.

Melissa Short had been correct, sort of. When the word got out in the media that trapping was still allowed in many states around the country, there were protests, mostly at universities here and there, against trapping of any kind.

The most outspoken protesters in the different states actually got some traction with lawmakers, but when the senators and representatives discovered that for the most part their constituents didn't really care about the issue, they let it go. They needed to spend their time, they believed, on figuring out what to do with the growing homeless populations in their cities, and the rocketing use of fentanyl and the deaths caused by the horrible drug.

Not that the issue had totally gone away. One day the following February, Luke was reading some wildlife crime reports from around the country, and he saw a tidbit about a trapper in Wisconsin who had found a bear trap set near his trapline. He thought it might have been meant for him.

Unbeknownst to the perpetrator, the trapper had placed some trail cameras along his trapline because he thought someone was purposefully springing his traps and stealing the bait. One of the cameras caught an interesting photo.

The photo that accompanied the article showed a man, who

Luke didn't recognize, and a tall, slender woman with long legs, long arms, and long hair braided into a rope, carrying the bear trap up the trail. He definitely recognized the woman and phoned the Fish and Wildlife Division of the Wisconsin Department of Natural Resources.

A sergeant with enforcement, a woman named Sandra Holt, answered and, after Luke identified himself and told her what he was calling about, he asked if they were still looking for the people in the photo.

"Yes, as a matter of fact we are," Holt said.

"Well, let me tell you a little story," Luke said.

And he did.

Acknowledgments

Special thanks to Ed Cunningham who suggested utilizing a trapping situation in an upcoming book. Ed also reviewed the book to make sure I wasn't way off base when it came to describing the traps and the trapping setups. I appreciate his time and knowledge.

Thanks, too, to my wife and sons—Terri, Kyle and Kevin—who read as I wrote this book, keeping me on course with advice and encouragement.

ABOUT THE AUTHOR

Rob is an award-winning outdoor writer and author of the bestselling and critically acclaimed Luke McCain mystery series set in the wilderness of Eastern Washington and featuring a fish & wildlife officer and his yellow Lab, Jack.

Rob and his wife, Terri, live in Yakima, Washington with their very spoiled Labrador retriever.

9 781957 607313